PENGUINDRUM

PENGUINDRUM

NOVEL

3

WRITTEN BY

Kunihiko Ikuhara
Kei Takahashi

Seven Seas Entertainment

PENGUINDRUM VOLUME 3

MAWARU-PENGUINDRUM Vol. 3
by IKUHARA KUNIHIKO/TAKAHASHI KEI/HOSHINO LILY
© 2012 IKUHARA KUNIHIKO/TAKAHASHI KEI/
GENTOSHA COMICS INC.
© 2012 ikunichawder/pingroup
All rights reserved.

Original Japanese edition published in 2012 by
GENTOSHA COMICS Inc.
English translation rights arranged worldwide with
GENTOSHA COMICS Inc. through Digital Catapult Inc., Tokyo.

Seven Seas press and purchase enquiries can be sent to
Marketing Manager Lianne Sentar at press@gomanga.com.
Information regarding the distribution and purchase of
digital editions is available from Digital Manager CK Russell
at digital@gomanga.com.

Seven Seas and the Seven Seas logo are trademarks of
Seven Seas Entertainment. All rights reserved.

Follow Seven Seas Entertainment online at
sevenseasentertainment.com.

TRANSLATION: Molly Lee
COVER DESIGN: Nicky Lim
INTERIOR LAYOUT & DESIGN: Clay Gardner
PROOFREADER: Kelly Lorraine Andrews, Stephanie Cohen
LIGHT NOVEL EDITOR: Nibedita Sen
PREPRESS TECHNICIAN: Rhiannon Rasmussen-Silverstein
PRODUCTION MANAGER: Lissa Pattillo
MANAGING EDITOR: Julie Davis
ASSOCIATE PUBLISHER: Adam Arnold
PUBLISHER: Jason DeAngelis

ISBN: 978-1-64505-541-9
Printed in Canada
First Printing: May 2021
10 9 8 7 6 5 4 3 2 1

33614082316067

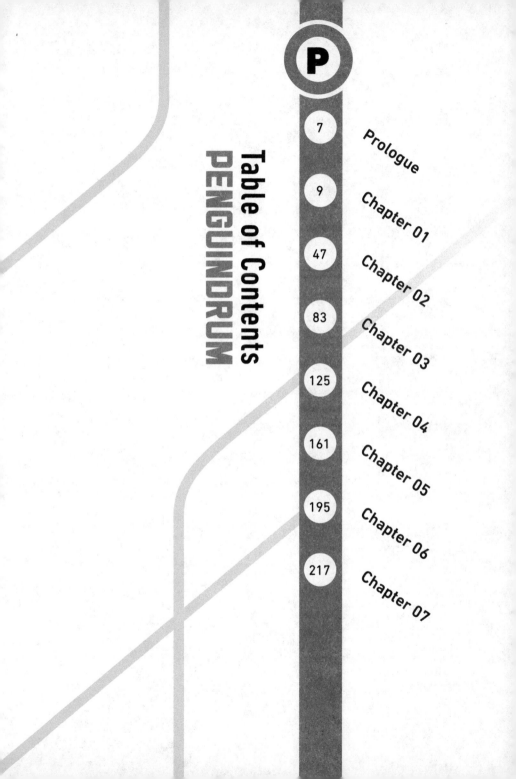

Table of Contents
PENGUINDRUM

7   Prologue

9   Chapter 01

47   Chapter 02

83   Chapter 03

125   Chapter 04

161   Chapter 05

195   Chapter 06

217   Chapter 07

PROLOGUE

•••→

YOU AWAKEN AS THE WORLD defrosts into a brand new season. The stopped clock begins to tick once more. At first, the solitude frightens you to tears and sends you into deep despair—you might even wish you could have stayed asleep. But no, everything happens for a reason. My love runs in your veins. And if ever you were loved, then you can't possibly be alone.

If you start singing with that soft little voice, the washed-out world around you will surely regain its color. A new flower will adorn your hair, and your cheeks will turn rosy pink. With the sweet scent wafting all around you, you'll step down onto the fresh green earth and leave your cold bed behind.

Truth be told, be it fate or be it a cursed connection, I wanted to stay by your side—to take you by the hand, tell you it'll be okay, and pull you into a reassuring hug. I wanted to share the scarlet fruit with you and keep your little heart beating. But we have a choice to make. At any given moment, we must choose the one single destiny we feel is best at the time. So let's just promise that no matter what happens, we won't regret it—a pinky promise to never cry over spilt milk. See? The cherry blossoms are in full bloom now, watching over you. Do not fear their gentle eyes.

No matter how alone you feel right now, you must open the door and move on. Someday you will reunite...and someday you will learn to love again.

CHAPTER 01

ON A COLD, WINDY NIGHT, Kanba sat at the bright red counter of a little ramen shop on the outskirts of town.

"Freakin' cold," he muttered, exhaling white fog. Both of his arms were bandaged nearly to the elbow. He shrank down into his black military jacket, burying his face in the matching black faux fur lining the collar.

"Have your hands healed?" a woman asked, concerned.

"Yeah. They look a lot worse than they actually are, but trust me, it's no big deal," he answered in an uncharacteristically calm, gentle voice.

"Kanba."

He felt a hand on his shoulder and turned to find Takakura Kenzan and Chiemi sitting beside him at the counter, gazing at him softly.

"You've been doing a truly wonderful job. You make your father proud," Kenzan whispered.

"You really are the perfect son," Chiemi chimed in, a soft smile playing at her lips as she reached out and stroked Kanba's short hair, ice-cold from exposure to the night wind. Bashfully, he smiled and stared down at the counter.

"We can't come home until our mission is complete, so you have to protect the Takakura family until then. Understand?"

Kenzan gazed at Kanba with a pained, yet unwavering look in his eyes. Kanba looked back at him with renewed resolve.

"Look out for Shoma and Himari, won't you?" Chiemi asked in a feeble voice.

"I will." His arms felt stiff—possibly from the cold—and ached more sharply than they had during the day.

"Give my son the usual," Kenzan told the man standing behind the counter, dressed all in black. The man set a thick envelope down in front of Kanba.

Everything would be fine. All Kanba had to do was keep putting out fires until Kenzan and Chiemi could return. Then, eventually, there would come a day when the entire Takakura family would reunite. They would all live together, and Shoma and Himari would never have to feel lonely ever again.

Wordlessly, Kanba slid the envelope into his jacket pocket.

Tabuki never came back to our school after that. The only closure we got was a brief morning announcement informing us that "Tabuki Keiju-sensei has formally resigned." His assistant was temporarily promoted into the newly vacated position, and one of the older teachers took over our biology class.

"Here you can see the chloroplasts inside the leaf of this plant. They harvest energy from sunlight and use it to synthesize glucose and other carbohydrates from water and carbon dioxide. This is how plants produce oxygen. The umbrella term is *photosynthesis*, but today we'll be looking at how this process can change under certain conditions."

Meanwhile, my classmates were gossiping about why Tabuki would suddenly quit his job, though nobody really questioned it. None of the students especially disliked him, but they were never all that interested in him, either. In the past, this was true for me and Kanba, too.

Just then, I heard loud whispers near the back of the classroom.

"So why did Tabuki quit, anyway?"

"Maybe he got sick of teaching at an all-boys' school."

"He seemed like a hard-working kind of guy. Maybe the stress got to him."

They were right—Tabuki was a hard-working guy. That was why, when pushed to the breaking point, he snapped and did the things he did.

I snuck a glance at Kanba. He was resting his chin in his palm and staring into space like he couldn't care less. His arms were still bandaged up, but you couldn't really see it through his uniform sleeves. I sighed and looked away.

"As for the process of transpiration, uh...I think we covered that last time, right? In that case, let's refer to the graph there in your textbooks. The x axis represents the absorption rate of carbon dioxide, while the y axis represents the intensity of sunlight.

This shows us how photosynthesis changes based on the light's brightness. Now, what does the x axis tell us? Anyone? How about you?" The teacher pointed at one of the gossiping students. "Can you tell us the answer?"

"Uhh...I don't know," the student answered in a small, sheepish voice.

"Okay then. Someone else?"

With a sigh, I decided I liked this new teacher.

Thanks for everything. I wish you well.

The words were written in stiff, angular handwriting on a scrap of paper on the living room table, placed alongside the key to the condo. Not only that, but the curtains Yuri brought home were now hanging from the curtain rods over each window. Unfortunately, this did little to improve the stark chill.

That morning, Yuri sat alone, drinking a warm cup of coffee and thinking about the halfway-planned reception, about Momoka, about the Takakura children. She sank back into the sofa, wearing slippers on her feet and a cardigan over her champagne-gold silk pajamas. The ring had vanished from her left hand, but that man was still her husband. So where had he gone?

Back in autumn, on the anniversary of Momoka's passing, Yuri had invited Tabuki to the first Indian restaurant she could think of. They sat on opposite sides of the table and ate beef curry over rice on plates garnished with raisins.

"Married?" he repeated, frowning, as he lowered his clean spoon back to the table.

"Yes, that's right. The two of us should stick together," she replied as if it was the obvious choice. Then she started in on her meal without waiting for him.

"You really think so?"

He shifted his gaze to the metal pot full of steaming hot curry. She cleared her throat, then took a sip of water.

"I do. You and I are connected through the Wheel of Fortune," she declared.

"Through Momoka, you mean?"

Indeed, Tabuki Keiju and Tokikago Yuri were the only two people who knew about Momoka's secret power—that much was certain. But Tabuki had no romantic feelings for Yuri, and as far as he knew, she didn't feel that way about him, either. No, what they truly loved was Momoka and the precious few moments they spent with her in childhood.

"If we become a family, we can be with Momoka forever."

Yuri believed this wholeheartedly. After all, Tabuki was the only other person who knew Momoka like she did. Together, they could spend their whole lives loving her.

"No. We could never be a family," Tabuki said.

Sure, they could fill out the paperwork and establish a legal connection between them, but *family* wasn't as simple as that. Tabuki was already sick to death of being bound and controlled by familial ties. All he needed was Momoka.

"As long as we act the part, it'll feel real eventually," Yuri had tried to persuade him. Tabuki had hesitated in the face of her stubborn optimism...but eventually, his thirst for revenge won out.

Sadly, their marriage hadn't lasted long.

"I suppose it was simply never going to work out for the two of us," Yuri mused to herself as she laid herself down on the sofa, clutching one half of the diary in her hand. "Perhaps it was impossible."

Was she stupid for wanting to have a family? Or friends? Could she have spared herself this strange sense of loneliness if she had simply searched for the diary by herself?

Yuri was surprised to realize that she was actually slightly worried about Tabuki. She always figured that if the relationship broke down, she would bounce back to her usual life of solitude without much trouble. Shrinking in the cold, she flipped through the half-diary all over again. But without its other half, it held no meaning. The fate-altering spell was incomplete.

"*Thank you for everything*, he says. For *what*, exactly?"

It was Tabuki who always got up and fetched her a cardigan or blanket when she was cold, and he was usually the one who took out the trash, too. He wouldn't drink with her, but sometimes he would dutifully sit with her while she partook. Their relationship could never quite be described as "family," but it still felt like it ended too soon.

Back to bed, she decided. After she awoke, she'd take a hot shower, then call the wedding venue to discuss their reservation. And after that, she'd need to get in touch with the fashion designer about her custom-ordered wedding dress.

I pulled three clear plastic clothing storage bins out of the closet, each lazily marked with a piece of red packing tape with a name written on it: *Kanba, Shoma, Himari.*

"Hey, Sho-chan, um...I can't seem to find my red sweater with the fuzzy buttons on the back," said Himari as she folded up all of her winter clothes side by side.

"Red sweater? I don't remember seeing one. Maybe it's in one of the other bins." Kanba and I had finished unpacking our winter clothes while Himari was still in the hospital, so our bins were filled with summer clothes instead. "I'm sure we must've come across it at some point, though."

Himari always took the longest to repack, which was why we made her go last.

"Times like these, I usually find it mixed in with Kan-chan's stuff..." She knelt down beside me and opened Kanba's bin.

"Yikes. Somebody ought to refold all that," I muttered before I could stop myself.

"It must still be painful for him to use his hands," she mused.

Indeed, though he was finally freed from his bandages, his wounds were still painful to look at. That being said, I was pretty sure none of that had anything to do with this slapdash folding job. No, this was proof of Kanba's personality—he simply went through the motions without actually paying attention to any of the minor details, like arrangement or wrinkle prevention. He would simply gesture at it and say, "There! Folded 'em!" And yes, technically, he was right.

"*Aha*! See? Told you so!" Smiling, Himari pulled her red sweater out from beneath Kanba's summer wear.

"Do you have everything now?" I asked, surveying the rainbow of colored cloth lying on the floor. She liked to keep wearing her summer clothes in layers during the other seasons, so her storage box was practically empty during the winter, unlike ours.

"Yup," she nodded with a satisfied grin. Penguin No. 3 nodded along sleepily amid the vast ocean of wool.

"Cool. Let's get everything set up before the others arrive."

Today we were planning to have sukiyaki to celebrate Himari's return from the hospital. Kanba was on grocery duty, while Himari and I were in charge of cooking. Not only that, Kanba and I made a construction-paper banner that read *WELCOME HOME HIMARI!*

"Wake up, San-chan! We're gonna have sukiyaki!"

As she moved her clothes into the dresser, she gave No. 3 a pat on the head. It opened its little button eyes a tiny crack and squeaked faintly.

We hadn't used the sukiyaki pot in a good long while, so I gave it a rewash to be on the safe side. Now it sat in the center of the table, surrounded by a medley of ingredients: green onions, shirataki noodles, shiitake mushrooms, grilled tofu, chop suey greens, and of course, the Takakura family's special homemade sukiyaki sauce, made by yours truly. Next to it sat the meat Kanba brought home from the store.

Gathered around the table, the four of us raised our cups.

"Welcome home, Himari!" Kanba and I shouted in unison.

"Welcome home, Himari-chan! I'm happy for you!" said Oginome-san with a smile.

"Thanks. But I'll still have to go back in for regular checkups," Himari replied with a shrug and a bashful smile. She was wearing the red sweater from earlier over a pair of jeans, and she'd tied her hair into loose pigtails.

"Eh, don't worry about it," Kanba grinned.

"Yeah. What matters is that you're home now," I chimed in as I greased the pot.

"From now on, you won't be lonely at mealtimes anymore! You ought to celebrate it!" Oginome-san insisted with a broad smile.

Earlier, when Himari asked me whether we should invite Oginome-san to dinner, I hesitated. Granted, I vowed to myself that I would stop running from her, but even then, I wasn't sure how she would react to me pulling a 180 and inviting her over out of nowhere. In the end, however, I was glad I did.

"Hey, um...thanks for coming over tonight."

"Are you kidding? I wouldn't miss Himari-chan's celebration! But I gotta say, this meat looks real expensive."

She looked down at the marbled sukiyaki beef. The rest of us followed suit.

"It's very aesthetically pleasing," Himari commented, her eyes sparkling.

"For the first time in my life, I ordered the most expensive cut of meat they had. I was so nervous, I was practically shaking in my boots," Kanba bragged.

"You got the most expensive one? How much per gram?" I asked, purely on reflex. Sure, I could tell at a glance that it was high quality, but the knowledge that it was *the best they had* made my wallet cringe.

"Don't be a cheapskate, all right? I got my paycheck from work, and I wanted to spend it on something special," he replied offhandedly.

"Aniki, you haven't been doing anything shady, have you?" I asked, halfway serious.

The room went silent.

"The hell do you mean, *shady*?"

"I...I don't know...working at a host club or something? You've been coming home really late at night for a while now."

I didn't *actually* think he was working at a host club, but knowing Kanba, he could easily find a way to pretend he was of legal age.

"What? Really?" Oginome-san's jaw dropped.

"Wait, so Kan-chan is a male entertainer?" Himari asked with a frown, holding Penguin No. 3 in her arms.

"No, stupid! Of course not!" Kanba snapped. Then he downed his entire cup of tea.

"You know, I bet Kanba-kun would do well in that line of work," Oginome-san mused thoughtfully. "He'd look really good in an all-white suit."

I thought back to the tense smile I'd seen on his face once upon a time.

"Hey, quit making stuff up about me! I'm not gonna wear some tacky suit, damn it. Now let's eat some meat! Shoma, get the eggs!"

"Well, okay. As long as your job isn't making you do anything shady, I won't pry."

As I spoke, I passed out bowls and eggs to each person in turn, then poured the sukiyaki sauce into the pot. As far as I could tell, I confirmed that Kanba wasn't working at a host club...but in that case, what kind of job was paying him this well?

"Oh, uh, guys? Before we get started on the meat, *someone's* got an important announcement to make," Oginome-san told us, shooting Himari a glance.

Nervously, Himari pursed her lips. Then she rose to her feet and disappeared into her room, returning moments later with a paper Yozawaya bag. She reached into it and pulled out two large parcels, each with a ribbon on top—one red, one blue.

"Kan-chan, Sho-chan, thank you for everything you do for me. Today, um...today's Sibling Appreciation Day," she explained, blushing faintly as she pushed the parcels into our hands.

"Can I open it now?" I asked.

"Of course!"

I pulled the blue ribbon loose, then unwrapped the parcel. Inside was a soft, brightly colored sweater.

"Whoa..."

"Oooh!" Beside me, Kanba admired the contents of his own parcel.

"Thank you, Himari! You were knitting these for us back in the hospital, weren't you?" *What a precious little angel.* I could feel my eyes burning.

"You were?" Kanba's jaw dropped.

"Uh huh. I wanted to surprise you, so I asked Ringo-chan to help me keep it a secret. Sorry for hiding it," Himari explained with a smile. "The size might be a little off, though. Can you try them on real quick?"

I plunged into the soft wool and slid my shirt-clad arms through the sleeves.

"It's perfect!"

The color was nicely accentuated by the raised rib stitches. The round neckline was the perfect size, too. All around, it was very soft and warm.

"How do you feel about the color and the design and stuff?"

"No, yeah, it's...it's pretty good. And toasty warm, too." Kanba stared at the floor in embarrassment—a rare sight.

"Oh, I'm so glad!" Himari's face lit up in a rosy smile.

"Looks like your surprise is a hit!" Oginome-san whispered into her ear. Smirking, Himari whispered something back.

"What's with the whisper party?" Kanba scowled.

"It's a secret."

"Ditto!"

Then they both started to giggle. They were so buddy-buddy, I couldn't help but laugh.

"Seriously, this sweater is really toasty. And it's so flawlessly made, too." I ran a hand down my chest, admiring the stitches.

"Guess what, Shoma-kun? I helped her pick out the yarn. We had a heck of a time finding a color that would look good on you!"

But I paid Oginome-san's flirtatious comments no mind. "Himari, I promise, I'll cherish this sweater for as long as I live. Thank you so much!" I exclaimed, wiping my tears away with one hand.

"Hey! Are you even listening?"

Yes, I was. I just didn't know how to respond. In all my life, I'd rarely ever worn my emotions on my sleeve, and I couldn't really picture myself changing that—couldn't picture myself treating her like a girlfriend, for example. So really, it was no wonder that Kanba and Yamashita always called me a late bloomer. Before I could think of some way to change the subject, however, she reached up and grabbed my head in her hands.

"Wha?! Ow ow ow ow!"

"I said, *are you listening*?!" Oginome-san sneered, pulling me in close. Himari burst out laughing, and Kanba let out a knowing chuckle.

Had we finally found peace? Had we successfully switched tracks on the railroad of fate? *I mean, just look at them.* Everyone was smiling—real, genuine, happy smiles.

After we polished off the udon and the pot was empty, Kanba laid himself down on the tatami beside the table. "Turns out pricey beef is totally worth it."

"Kan-chan, you shouldn't lie down right after a meal or you'll turn into a cow."

Himari ate more than usual this time, slipping meat to the penguins when no one else was looking. Now she was humming cheerfully to herself.

"Mooooo," he responded from the floor.

"Okay then..." I started to stack up the dirty dishes. Oginome-san quietly joined in.

"Wait, Ringo-chan! I can do that!" Himari moved to get up.

"No, no, that's okay. You're our VIP tonight, Himari-chan. You're allowed to sit back and relax for a change." With a smile, Oginome-san carried all the dishes to the sink.

I pulled on my apron and got to work, first filling the dishpan with warm water, then getting out my scrub brush and sponges (one for oily dishes only, and one for everything else). Of these, I grabbed the scrub brush first.

"Can I put this here?" Oginome-san asked casually.

"Sure. Thanks," I replied with a smile. "I'll do the oily dishes first, since I want to get this pot out of the way."

"Okay, then I'll wash the rest."

"Oh, okay. If you want, you can use that apron over there." I pointed to the pink apron that Himari usually liked to wear.

"You're really good at cleaning, huh?" she asked as she watched me work.

"I'm just used to doing it every day," I replied.

"Thank you for inviting me, Shoma-kun," she continued in a small voice as she stood beside me. "I didn't think you would, but..."

"Can't have a party without guests, right? Besides, Himari wanted to see you. Really, don't worry about it."

"What about you?"

"What?"

"Did *you* want to see me?"

"Yeah."

The word left my lips so fast, it sounded more like *yah*. Out of the corner of my eye, I saw Oginome-san's face light up.

"Glad to hear it."

Himari sat in Sanetoshi's exam room, rebuttoning her blouse with an unusually morose look on her face. Shirase and Souya stood in their nurse uniforms, observing her gloom with puzzlement.

Sanetoshi pulled off his stethoscope and set it on the desk. "Stunning, wasn't it? Eating dinner with the family, like old times?" he asked as he scribbled notes in her chart.

"Yeah," Himari answered absently.

"Is something the matter?" He looked up at her. A translucent blue ring spread into the air just overhead.

"I figured it out. You sent me home because my illness can't be cured, right?"

"A carefully constructed theory. What makes you think that?" He smiled dryly, his eyelashes glittering.

"It's just so obvious! Why else would you discharge me when you keep having to increase my dosage? I'm going to die, aren't I?"

"Of course not," he answered flatly.

"You're lying," she shot back firmly.

"Then what do you want me to say?" he asked—not harshly, but not quite as warmly as before.

"I'm sorry. I guess I'm just being paranoid," she said with a forced smile.

"Tell me the truth," Sanetoshi said.

Instantly, her smile vanished. A chill ran down her spine, as if his question reached directly into her heart. Somehow it felt as though he knew exactly what she was secretly worried about.

"The truth?"

"The whole truth."

She hesitated for a moment...then began to explain.

"Well, you see...I'm starting to feel like I don't belong with my family anymore."

It all started when she saw Ringo standing in the kitchen, doing *her* chores, wearing *her* apron, smiling at Shoma. Himari already knew how the two of them felt about each other, and normally she would've been supportive, but...at the time, she couldn't help but feel like Ringo had replaced her. And she couldn't bear to see Shoma smiling back at her stand-in.

It felt like everyone was going to leave her behind all over again.

"I hate this. Why do I feel this way when they're nothing but kind and considerate to me?"

"You don't belong with them, hmm? Where *do* you belong, then? What is it you want to do?"

On the wall of the dimly lit exam room, the hands of the projected clock began to slowly spin backwards.

"I want everything to stay the same. Just me and Kan-chan and Sho-chan forever."

Not that she held a grudge against Ringo, of course. And while it felt like the part of her that originally welcomed Ringo into the group was actually a lying witch the entire time, like it or not, this was the whole truth.

"Are you sure that's what you want?" Sanetoshi asked casually.

"What?"

"You're afraid that when you come to terms with how you truly feel, it will destroy something that means a lot to you. Isn't that right?"

"What are you talking about? I'm being honest with you."

"Are you, though? For I have no insight regarding your feelings, or your truth, or your past."

He smiled faintly, and the projected clock froze entirely. The light imbued within his hair slowly shifted from blue to purple.

Himari knew that she was not the pure-hearted girl she pretended to be, but she had grown tired of forcing a smile at all times. This was the most honest she could possibly be...and yet, for some reason, she felt a deep sense of unease within her chest. For the entire duration of the subway ride home, she clutched Penguin No. 3 tightly in her lap, squeezing its short, soft feathers between her fingers as she stroked its head. On the opposite side of the car, she could see her reflection in the window, looking slightly too pale but otherwise no different from usual.

"My true feelings," she murmured absently to herself as she gazed out the window at the darkening scenery, swaying with the motions of the train. "My truth...my past..."

If there was some sort of *secret truth* deep in her brain, or the bottom of her heart, or at the very core of her being—a secret even Himari herself knew nothing about—then how could she have forgotten it?

There were *dozens* of meaningful things she didn't want

destroyed; she couldn't possibly figure out which in particular Sanetoshi was referring to.

Lots of troubled visitors today. Smiling, Sanetoshi gazed at Masako, who stared coldly back.

"Surely *you're* not feeling under the weather, too, are you? Shall I examine you?" he teased.

"Tell me: what is the significance of the incantation written here?" she asked, holding her half of the diary.

"There is none," he answered without missing a beat. "It's no different from 'open sesame.' The words themselves have no meaning."

"I beg your pardon? What, so it's just *magic*?" She seemed slightly unnerved.

"Precisely. By completing the incantation, you will save your brother's life and reroute his fate."

"Are you joking? You're a doctor," she scoffed. "This must be a metaphor for pharmaceutical development or something, right?"

"I'm afraid you're mistaken," he replied, offhanded as always.

"So you're saying—?"

"I'm a wizard," he declared with a grin.

The stool creaked as Masako leapt to her feet, enraged. "So you're saying you never had any intention of helping us, right from the outset?!"

What self-respecting doctor would call himself a wizard? "Completing the incantation"? What kind of fairytale world was he living in?

"Now if you had both halves of the diary, it'd be a different story," he shrugged.

"Liar! What are you after? What's your angle?"

"I want to fix this broken world," he answered matter-of-factly, a faint smile playing at his lips. On the wall, the hands of the projected clock began to warp and twist.

"*Liar!*" she repeated, clutching the diary tightly as she glared at him.

"It's the truth."

For a moment, his expression turned serious, and the plantlike smell that wafted from his hair grew stronger. Dizzy, Masako pressed her free hand over her eyes and thought back to the dream she had about the subway train. Hadn't Sanetoshi told her about the world? And Kanba was there, too...but then he abandoned her and Mario. She remembered watching him and her father walk away from her, both of them dressed in black.

"What are you forcing Kanba to do?"

She wasn't expecting an answer to this. She believed it was all a dream—that it was as fictional as magic.

"Your parents failed to make their dream come true. So instead, I'm going to pass that duty down to their children."

Frowning, she scrutinized his face in profile—specifically, the upturned tip of his nose. As far as she knew, there was only one "dream" he could be referring to. But that was no *dream*. It was an old scar that ran deep.

"Stop it! I won't allow it!" Masako roared, shoulders heaving.

"You refuse to board the train of fate?" Sanetoshi asked, raising his eyebrows.

"Yes, that's right. And I won't let Kanba on board, either!" she declared. Then she whipped the door open and stormed out of the exam room. At last, she had put into words what she felt on the morning after she awoke from the dream.

Left behind in the exam room, Sanetoshi gestured with one hand, as if to say *get a load of that*.

"She sure was mad," Shirase giggled.

"Steaming mad," Souya chimed in.

"Mad enough to go home and throw the diary in the fire, perhaps. I'd do it myself if I could," Sanetoshi smirked smugly. Then he spun in his chair and looked up at the clock projected on the wall. It must have un-warped itself at some point while they were talking.

"You're a genius!"

"It's stunning!"

"As long as that thing's floating around, I can't win the game," he muttered in a low drawl, as if in a trance.

Masako sat on the very edge of the armchair, her posture perfectly straight. As she gazed at the fireplace heating the living room, she pressed a finger to the diary in her lap. If it wasn't for this stupid thing, that doctor wouldn't have started talking about nonsense like magic and incantations, and the topic of Kanba wouldn't have come up, either. She didn't know how competent Sanetoshi was at his job, but she could tell that he was up to no good. So if he wanted the diary, then perhaps she was better off burning it to ashes—that way he would never get what he wanted. A fitting punishment for lying to her.

She stared at the fire dancing within its sturdy brick constraints. If she fed the diary to the flames, it would turn to ash in moments, never to be reunited with its other half.

"What do you think, Esmeralda?" she asked, without turning to look at the penguin lounging on the sofa nearby. "Tell me: are *you* made of magic and incantations and all that?"

Esmeralda looked at Masako's conflicted expression with its narrow little eyes. It blinked several times, all without making a peep.

"But...what if I really do need this to save Mario-san?"

In that case, she couldn't possibly burn it.

She thought back to Mario sleeping peacefully in his bedroom, his ghostly pale complexion, his long eyelashes, his neatly trimmed blond hair... From time to time, his lips would twist and tremble as he gasped for air. Why wasn't Kanba around for them at a time like this? How could he possibly turn a blind eye to them? Infuriating as it was, Masako knew the reason for a long time now.

Takakura Himari took up residence in Kanba's heart. She showed no signs of trying to curry his favor, and yet there she was, openly enjoying it. But as long as she and the rest of that family had their claws in him, Kanba would never return home to Masako.

"Goodness. I'd better crush them soon," she whispered, rather than letting her tears fall. The flames were so bright and red, they made her eyes hurt, but she squinted at them nonetheless.

Before we even boarded the subway train, the sky outside was covered in a blanket of gray clouds. The temperature was slowly dropping all day, and I could tell it was going to rain. This was slightly different from what the morning forecast promised.

"I wonder how long this can last."

After another peaceful day at school with no sign of Tabuki anywhere, we boarded the subway train and headed home to Himari—happy times with just the three of us.

"It'll last forever. No matter what happens, I'll protect the Takakura family," Kanba declared without looking at me.

But I wasn't so sure. Where had Tabuki Keiju gone? If I let myself believe that it was all over, it felt like fate was going to pull the rug right out from under me.

"What if something like that happens again?"

"Relax. I've already taken the punishment myself." He looked down at the deep scars in his palms.

Fortunately, no harm befell Himari—but Kanba was hurt in the process. At the time, I was powerless to do anything; without Oginome-san there, I might have lost it completely. Why did it have to happen? I was trying my best to come to terms with the reality of my past and present, but nevertheless, every day was a struggle.

"It's all *their* fault," I muttered, and Kanba glanced at me. "Mom and Dad, I mean."

I met his gaze. He looked at me with a hint of confusion in his eyes.

"I'll never forgive them. I mean, think about it! Tabuki's not the only victim—there's *tons* of people who hold a grudge against us to this very day. And our parents are responsible for all of it. Even Himari's—"

"Don't go there," he cut in quietly to stop me.

I swallowed my words, then rephrased them: "We don't need them, do we?"

Our parents were nowhere to be seen, but we could still get by without them, so clearly we had no need of them. As long as Himari stayed healthy and we all stayed together, we didn't need anything else.

"No, we don't," he replied curtly. His voice was so low, the vibration of the train was nearly enough to drown it out.

Ideally, I wanted to get home before the rain hit. I didn't have any plans for tonight's dinner, but I could probably think of something once I got to the grocery store and saw what was on sale. Something warm and hearty for the winter season.

Thunder rumbled from deep within the dusky gray clouds. Himari lay in bed with Penguin No. 3, flipping through the Takakura family photo album. The penguin peered curiously at each page.

"These are from when we went to the aquarium. You recognize it, right? We've got one of them framed in the living room."

This particular page was covered in photos of the three

Takakura siblings when they were kids. With each turn of the page, they grew younger and younger.

"We really haven't changed a bit, have we?"

Her heart fluttered as she realized what she'd said. *My true feelings...my truth...my past...* Could she really claim that no one changed?

"And here's us at the beach...and here's the amusement park. I was really little, so there were a lot of rides I wasn't allowed to go on. The haunted house let me in, though. But it was pitch-black inside, and I was scared stiff!"

She and Shoma had both clung to Kanba as they made their way through the spooky attraction. She could remember the chilly air tickling her ankles. Kanba had tried to shrug it off like it was no big deal, but he was pretty clearly bluffing, since his palms were sweaty. But despite her fear, Himari never once regretted taking the plunge. She had vowed to enjoy every single attraction that would let all three of them inside.

When they finally reached the exit, they were met with warm, bright sunshine. Their parents were waiting for them, smiling as they watched their terrified children scramble outside. Himari dashed right over to her mother and clung to her legs.

"Oh, good heavens. You should have let me come with you like I suggested," Chiemi chided her gently.

"What a lame haunted house. It wasn't even scary!" Kanba scoffed, putting up a tough front.

"You okay, Himari?" Shoma asked, running over to her as she clung to their mother in silence. "It's all over now, okay?"

Kenzan held up his camera. "All right, kids, now let's take a photo in honor of your courage."

Then the three children lined up in front of the sign advertising the haunted house, their expressions an odd mix of fear and relief. The memory made Himari laugh. Of course they had changed—they had no option not to. The three of them had come a long way, and there was no going back for any of them. Almost like they were shipwrecked on a tiny deserted island far, far away.

"I wish Sho-chan and Kan-chan would hurry up and come home already." It looked like it was going to rain any minute, and she could think of fewer things more unpleasant than commuting home in wet clothes.

Just then, the doorbell rang. Himari sprang out of bed and dashed off to the door, leaving the open photo album behind. She knew her brothers would never bother to ring the doorbell before coming in—so who could be paying her a visit on this chilly evening?

"Who is it?"

When she opened the sliding door, there stood Masako with a hard look on her face, her curls perfectly styled, wearing a classy camel-colored leather trench coat, black tights, and black high-heeled ankle boots.

"Goodness. I'd better crush you soon," said Masako with a frown. Then she reached up and pressed a hand to the crease in her brow. Her neatly trimmed nails were the color of blood blisters.

"Uhhh...?"

Himari could smell sensual, sweet perfume mixed in with the chilly air. This total stranger had the most beautiful almond-shaped eyes she had ever seen.

"Please accept this small trifle." Masako thrust the box she was holding in Himari's direction. Then she raised her head and took a whiff of the house's interior. "I take it Kanba isn't home?"

"Not at the moment..."

"Pardon my intrusion."

In a blink, Masako unzipped her boots, set them neatly beside the other shoes in the entryway, and walked inside.

"Wait! Um...we have slippers!" Himari offered, still holding the gift box. But Masako ignored her and scanned the tiny little living room. Then she strode over to the bright red sofa and sat down without removing her rain-soaked coat. Crossing her legs, she took in the childishly decorated sliding doors, the frayed pull cords on the lighting fixtures, the tissue box cover, the peach-pink curtains, and the clutter of unfamiliar toys lined up all over the TV and shelves.

"What a tacky house," she muttered. "How long does he intend to live in this run-down shack?"

"Thank you for the pudding. Would you like some?"

Himari returned to the coffee table with two cups of roasted green tea and two cups of pudding from Masako's gift box. Then she sat down on the opposite side, facing the sofa. This woman seemed to be looking for Kanba, and the displeasure on her face made Himari uneasy.

"Whatever Kan-chan did, I'm really sorry!" she blurted on reflex, bowing her head.

"What are you talking about?"

After seeing her up close, Masako could only conclude that Himari was a child. Her little head, her little braids, her little stick legs... She was wearing a pink wool cardigan over a gauzy blue shirt, denim shorts, and long, thick socks.

"Deep down, Kan-chan has a heart of gold. He's just...um...a bit of a womanizer," Himari continued, looking up at Masako. "But he doesn't mean any harm by it. I'm sure he never wanted to hurt you."

"I'm afraid I don't know what you're referring to. I just came to retrieve what is rightfully mine." *Detestable little wench,* Masako thought to herself.

"Huh? Did you give him a really pricey gift or something?"

"Oh, I've given him *plenty* of gifts over the years," she muttered, a distant look in her eyes. "But he rejected every one of them."

Himari wracked her brain, trying to think of the most expensive thing that Kanba acquired recently. Eventually she settled on: "Wait...you mean...the sukiyaki beef...?!"

"Excuse me?"

"I...I'm so sorry! I think he might have used your gift to buy sukiyaki meat!" she blurted in a panic.

"I seriously doubt that," Masako sighed. Perhaps the years spent living in this cluttered mess had turned the poor girl's brain into a cluttered mess as well.

"Okay, then it might still be around here somewhere! I'll go look for it. What, um...what did you give him?" Himari asked, rising to her feet.

"My love," Masako replied with a straight face.

Himari's eyes widened as her jaw dropped. Silence descended over the living room.

"I, uh...I might not be able to find it, then," she conceded in a small voice.

Masako was the first person she'd ever known to say the word "love" outright. And seeing as she was involved with Kanba, she was clearly a very mature person. Perhaps this sort of drama was par for the course when you were a womanizer.

"No. I *demand* that you return it."

As Himari's uncertainty grew, Masako became ever more convinced that she was unworthy of Kanba. This girl had no understanding of love.

"Well, if it's a matter of love, then it's up to Kan-chan to handle. I'm just his sister—I have no right to decide," Himari explained, attempting to strike a careful balance between courtesy and sincerity.

"His *sister*? Funny joke," Masako snorted.

"Uh, no, I'm not joking! I really am his sister! If you think I'm his girlfriend, then you're mistaken!"

"No, *you're* mistaken, Himari-san," Masako shot back without missing a beat.

Himari looked at her sharply. *How does she know my name?* Had Kanba told her?

"Your arrogance truly knows no bounds, it seems. You make my skin crawl... You're not even his real family," Masako continued.

Himari wanted to refute this statement, but she was having a hard enough time just remembering to breathe. *What is she doing here? Why does she know my name? And why would she say that?*

"It's because of your little sister act that Kanba refuses to come home to me."

"Little sister act?" Himari repeated. She wasn't putting on an "act" at all. But for some reason, uncertainty flared up in her chest, swiftly transforming into terror.

"Give Kanba back to me! You cannot build reality out of fiction!" Masako roared.

Himari flinched and took a few steps backward. "Leave. Now. Please." She looked down at her feet and swallowed hard, her lips trembling. There stood a little black penguin looking smugly back at her, its eyes as narrow as its owner's.

"San-chan!" she whimpered desperately. At this, Penguin No. 3 peeked out from Himari's bedroom. The blood drained from its face as it looked at her. When their eyes met, it dashed over and hid itself behind Himari's legs.

"Oh, have you forgotten? Very well then. Allow me to jog your memory." Calmly, Masako pulled out her trusty slingshot gun and red golf-ball bullets. "These are custom-made Reminder Bullets! I'm going to make you remember who you really are!"

She aimed the gun at Himari, who reflexively squeezed her eyes shut.

"Don't avert your eyes," Masako told her in an eerily calm voice. "Who are you? Why are you here? What do you want?"

Himari slowly opened her eyes, avoiding Masako's gaze. "I..."

Outside, rain began to fall from the muggy sky. The downpour swiftly grew heavier and heavier until the living room was overwhelmed with the sound and smell of rain.

What did I ever do to her? Himari wondered dazedly as she stared down the barrel of Masako's gun. For a moment, the two polar opposites froze, taking in each other's unwavering eyes.

Right as we were nearly home, carrying all the ingredients we'd need to make stew, it suddenly started pouring down rain. I handed the groceries to Kanba, then dashed all the way around to the backyard to retrieve the laundry hanging out to dry.

"We're home, Himari! It's raining!" I shouted, my arms laden with clean clothes, as I kicked off my loafers and stepped onto the porch. Then I opened the sliding glass door, stepped through the curtain, and entered the living room. I could see her standing there, looking tense. "You really need to keep the doors locked while we're gone. What's wrong?"

Then I followed her gaze to find Natsume Masako standing in front of the red sofa, pointing a gun at my sister.

"Aah! AAAAHH!"

"Of all the rotten timing... If we'd just been a little bit faster, we coulda made it home ahead of the rain," Kanba grumbled as he walked in through the front door at that exact same moment. Then he noticed the situation happening in the living room and froze.

The other girl took one look at Kanba and hesitated...but quickly turned back to Himari. "Your forehead is toast!"

Then, before we could stop her, she aimed her gun at Himari and fired. With a shriek, Himari narrowly dodged the bright red bullet.

"What are you doing?!"

I tried to run to my sister, but tripped over Penguin No. 2 and fell to the floor in a multi-colored explosion of fabric. Panicked, Himari ran barefoot out into the backyard.

"Himari!"

"What are *you* doing here?!" Kanba demanded of Masako.

"I came to get what's mine. My love! My past! My truth!"

He reached out to grab the arm that was holding the gun, but she smacked him away, jumped over me, and ran out into the rain after Himari.

"Hey! Wait!"

Hastily, I jumped to my feet and ran after her. The rain was beating down harder than ever, threatening to drown out my voice. When I arrived at the empty lot next door, I found Himari standing frozen in place, soaked to the skin, while Masako held her at gunpoint. Kanba ran past me toward them.

"Stop it, Masako!"

"Stay out of this! You know these Reminder Bullets aren't the only weapon in my arsenal!"

He slowed to a stop; the words "Reminder Bullets" made the breath catch in his throat. With a name like that, one hit was surely enough to dredge up old memories. Masako was attempting to regain her truth by bringing it all to light.

"I want what was stolen from me."

In spite of the pouring rain, her curls held firm. The slingshot gun made a clicking sound in her hand.

"Who *are* you?" Himari asked, her breath leaving her lips in a white fog, her voice shaky and hoarse.

"Who I am isn't important. It's finally time to crush you. You're going to remember everything! There will be no escaping the truth!"

A red laser sight affixed itself to Himari's forehead. Meanwhile, I was frozen in terror, unable to think of a way to stop her. Surely my brother and I would be able to take her on together...but I couldn't quite get a read on her.

"Himari, duck!" I screamed as loud as I could manage.

In the same moment, Kanba shot off like a bullet and slammed into Natsume Masako in a full-body tackle. Together, they fell to the muddy, rain-soaked ground. As for her bullet, it grazed past Himari, who was crouched down with her face in her hands, and embedded itself in the concrete wall behind her. As the rain poured down, she looked up at me dazedly, and our eyes met.

"Himari?" I asked quietly.

But before she could speak, she closed her eyes and passed out.

"Himari!" I raced over to her and lifted her into my arms.

"Why?!" Masako screeched as she rose to her feet.

She loaded her gun with bullets of a different color, then aimed the gun at us. But her footing was unsteady, and her eyes were red...with tears. Kanba stood there in silence, shielding Himari and me.

"Get out of the way, please. Like I said before, I can and will shoot you, Kanba."

Her voice was firm, but her cheeks were wet—from rain or tears, I could scarcely tell. Kanba remained silent.

"This is absurd. You know this little fake family can't possibly last forever, right?" she asked, pointing the gun in his direction. But *I* was the one who answered her.

"Our family isn't fake."

"You do realize you might be the only one who feels that way?" she snorted, looking in my direction without moving a muscle.

"We're a real family."

My chest ached. No, I wasn't the only one who felt this way. She was just trying to rattle me. I couldn't let her get under my skin.

"I refuse to accept this," she declared. Then, with a glance at Kanba, she lowered the gun and walked off into the rain, her black tights sopping wet.

After she was gone, I realized that my shoulders were so tense, I nearly forgot to breathe. I exhaled, then inhaled again deeply on reflex, pulling the icy air into my lungs until I started to cough. I heard the sound of a car door close, followed by the rumble of an engine.

"I guess she's gone," Kanba muttered flatly, his back still turned, staring in the direction in which she left.

It doesn't matter what SHE thinks. We're a family, I thought to myself over and over and over. But I wasn't brave enough to ask Kanba for reassurance.

"Sho-chan..." In my arms, Himari opened her eyes a crack.

"Himari, are you okay? Are you hurt?"

"It's not healthy for her to be out in the cold. Let's get back inside," said Kanba. He pulled his uniform jacket off and draped it over her upper body. Once he hoisted her up into his arms, he shot me a look.

"My soul mate..." With a faint smile, Himari reached out and touched my cheek with her pale, frozen fingertips.

"Huh?"

That Reminder Bullet didn't hit her, right? Then she closed her eyes and went back to sleep, snoring quietly—too quietly for my liking.

"We should draw her a bath," I said, my voice cracking, as if I hadn't heard a word she said. Then I dashed into the house, ran to the bathroom, and when my feet finally reached the cold tile floor, I reached up and touched my stiffened face.

Then I turned on the bathtub faucet, twisting the handle as far as it would go. The thunderous stream of water joined in a chorus with the patter of the rain, blocking out my every thought. I needed to bounce back to my normal self, fast. Then I needed to put Himari in the tub, get the stew started, and fold up that clean laundry. I shot a glance at Penguin No. 2, standing beside me like my loyal pet, then let out a heavy sigh.

I couldn't shake the earthy smell of nature from my nostrils, and it pained my heart.

As Himari lay collapsed on the muddy earth, rapidly losing consciousness, she felt the cold rain seep into her clothes—into her bones. And then she remembered her truth.

She could recall a large, rusty fan creakily spinning up above her. Everywhere she looked, she was surrounded by children who all looked to be about the same age as her. They all sat with their knees tucked up to their chins, dead-eyed and haggard. She adjusted the striped scarf wrapped around her neck and perked up her ears, eavesdropping on the conversation behind her.

"Where are we?" a mournful voice asked. *New kid,* Himari thought to herself.

"You don't know? This is the place where unwanted children are thrown away," another child answered in a low, matter-of-fact tone of voice. It was the kind of levelheaded response that suggested the one who said it had already given up on the world.

"And we're the unwanted children," Himari murmured, reconfirming to herself something she already knew full well.

"If you stay here long enough, you'll turn invisible and disappear."

"Disappear? For real?" the new kid asked, shocked and slowly losing hope.

"Yeah, for real. You'll get colder and colder, and then once your heart's frozen solid, it'll shatter into a billion pieces and you'll turn invisible."

Himari looked up and saw tidy rows of giant shredder blades floating all around them, glinting as they spun. Those blades would crush the unwanted children into pulp and render them invisible to the world. With a shrug, she buried her face in her scarf and pressed a hand to her chest in hopes of calming herself down. Even if she vanished, she would surely still get to keep this scarf. She had nothing to fear.

"I never amounted to anything, so now this is goodbye."

Without a sound, the ground under her suddenly transformed into a conveyor belt, shuttling all the children in a downward spiral toward the shredder. Himari quietly closed her eyes and attempted to keep her mind as blank as possible.

"Stop!" a familiar voice called out in the distance. But it wasn't fuzzy like an auditory hallucination—no, it was right there. "Don't do it! Don't go!"

"Who's there?" Himari called out into the empty air, her eyes wide.

"It's me! I'm here to take you home!" Just like that, the voice was suddenly right beside her; she could feel it against her skin.

"What home? I have no home."

Then the owner of the face leaned right up to her face and shouted: "You're coming back to my house with me! We're going to be a family!"

"But how? I'm not related to you."

If only I was, she thought to herself. But it was merely a wish, and even if there *was* a God out there, she knew well enough that He wouldn't hear her prayers. But then the owner of the voice turned her entire world upside-down.

"It'll work out. We've got magic on our side." The boy held up a shiny red apple for her to see. "Now let's share the fruit of fate."

As she struggled to process this, a ray of hope shone down, lighting her world anew.

"Thank you for choosing me."

As Himari rose to her feet, the ground was no longer a conveyor belt carrying her to annihilation inside the shredder. They were standing in a grassy field awash with the invigorating smell of flowers; the Child Broiler was nowhere to be seen. And the young boy standing in front of her, smiling softly? It was Shoma. He gently placed the apple in her little palm.

His smile hadn't changed a bit, nor had his soft, messy hair. He was no knight in shining armor, nor was he a god; he wasn't even particularly strong or handsome or rich. Nevertheless, he chose to stay with her. He gave her a place to belong. He was always there to lead her by the hand or stroke her hair.

Himari's truth...Himari's secret past...was Shoma, the boy with whom she shared the fruit of fate.

"He's my soul mate."

Back then, Kanba was not yet a member of the Takakura house.

PENGUINDRUM

CHAPTER 02 •••→

SLOWLY, I OPENED MY EYES and breathed in the smell of the chilly tatami. It was now so cold, getting out of bed was a struggle every morning. I lay under my blanket in a daze for a while, then summoned my resolve and leapt out to confront the winter chill. In the process, I accidentally kicked Penguin No. 2 and sent him rolling across the floor, still sound asleep. Shivering, I switched on the TV to get the weather forecast: sunny all day, allegedly. While I was at it, I went ahead and shook Kanba's shoulders while he lay in the futon next to mine, but I knew it wouldn't be enough to actually wake him.

Alone, I stepped into the chilly kitchen. Then, before I started making breakfast, I reached into the cupboard under the gas range and pulled out our parents' bowls and chopsticks, all wrapped up in newspaper like precious treasures...or revolting eyesores, take your pick. Careful not to make a sound, I lined them up beside the sink: two pairs of dark brown chopsticks of differing lengths, and two big, round bowls painted pale green on the outside and white on the inside, with a lotus flower sketched in gold at the bottom of each one. Frankly, it was terrifying just how nostalgic the sight of them made me feel.

As I crumpled up the old, yellowing newspaper, I took a deep breath. Then I grabbed the bowls and chopsticks and dropped them into the trash can. As the lid closed after them, I heard a dull *thud* as they hit the bottom—not quite enough for them to break.

Later, as the three of us set the table, I found myself glancing back at the trash can again and again. It felt like the bowls were quietly watching over us. But I didn't regret a thing...or so I continued to tell myself.

"Breakfast time!"

We all pressed our hands together to say grace. Then Kanba and I reached out to take the slightly burnt rolled omelets for ourselves. Himari watched us intently.

"How does it taste?"

"Pretty good!" Kanba grinned. He was already wearing his uniform, which was a bit unusual, and he looked like he was feeling refreshed.

"Yeah, it's good," I chimed in.

"Really? What a relief!" Himari exclaimed. Then she took a piece for herself and popped it into her mouth.

For some reason the two of them woke up early this morning and invaded my kitchen to make rolled omelets and pickled veggies. On my left, Kanba chopped up all the lettuce and eggplants we left in the fridge, while on my right, a sleepy-looking Himari whisked her eggs, wearing a robe over her nightgown. Sandwiched between them, I suppressed my restlessness and tried to focus on making the miso soup. Something told me none of us got a full night's sleep last night.

Yesterday, after we warmed Himari up in the bath, we put her to bed. Then, instead of stew, I made her favorite rice and veggie soup, lightly seasoned, with a beaten egg mixed in at the end. Back in the living room, the rain blew in onto the clean laundry. As for Kanba and myself, neither of us really knew what to say to each other, so we just talked about whatever immediately came to mind.

Stuff like, "Sucks about the laundry."

Stuff like, "I forget—do we have homework due tomorrow?"

By the end, we started debating why exactly Yamashita failed to get a girlfriend. But it never stopped feeling uncomfortable, and we ended up going to bed a lot earlier than usual. Lying there under my blanket in the darkened living room, I sighed so hard, it made my throat sting. *Everything will be back to normal in the morning,* I told myself over and over as I squeezed my eyes shut.

"Himari, how'd you get so good at cooking all of a sudden?" Kanba asked, his appetite as voracious as ever.

"I practiced in my head while I was in the hospital," Himari explained proudly.

"Your *imagination* helped you learn how to cook?!" Mine wasn't especially creative, so I couldn't picture myself having the same results.

"Dude, don't get jealous just because hers are better than yours."

"I'm not jealous!" I pouted. Then I shot Himari a look. She was smiling and sharing her rolled omelets with the penguins.

"Now try some of these pickled veggies. Made 'em myself."

"All you did was put them in a Ziploc and squeeze them…"

That said, they certainly *looked* how they were supposed to, at the very least.

"There's a trick to how you gotta squeeze 'em. It's my *special technique*." He wiggled his fingers suggestively.

"What are you pretending to squeeze? Because it sure doesn't look like pickles! Quit being a perv first thing in the morning!" I shouted, leaning across the table to glare at him.

"What are you talking about? What's perverted about it?" he shot back, unwavering.

Giggling, Himari took a sip of her soup. "Mmmm… Sho-chan, your miso soup tastes just like Mom's."

She didn't mean any harm by it, but we both fell silent. Sensing that something was amiss, she slowly set her bowl back on the table and stared at the floor.

Despite everything Natsume Masako said, we were a family. But Himari was acting strangely last night—that much was undeniable. I could remember the feeling of her cold, wet fingers brushing my cheek…her damp eyes gazing at me with warm affection…and we all knew what meaning lay behind it. The bright red Reminder Bullet never struck her, and yet somehow she remembered that our familial bond was as fragile as a sweet French meringue.

Nevertheless, I decided that we were still a family in spite of that. I decided to stop pretending not to notice the anger and resentment I felt toward my parents.

"Stop it, Himari," I told her in a small voice. "The Takakura family doesn't have a mom."

She looked up, seemingly with half a mind to say something, but no words left her faintly parted lips.

"He's right," Kanba muttered in a low voice.

Himari looked hurt for a moment, but regardless, I didn't amend my statement. This was the one thing I couldn't deny any longer. I couldn't forgive my parents, and I couldn't keep defending them, either.

"How are you feeling today, Himari? Any fever?" I asked calmly.

"No, I'm okay. I checked," she answered in a tiny voice.

"You have a doctor's appointment today, right? Be safe," I continued. Anything to keep the conversation going.

"I will."

I was hoping Kanba would make some kind of joke to lighten the mood, but was ultimately left disappointed. And so we ate the rest of our breakfast in silence, the only sound that of clinking silverware. Over time, I started to think maybe I messed up.

Feeling guilty and miserable, I left the house along with Kanba. But as far as I knew, I didn't say anything wrong...did I?

After a routine medical examination, Himari sat across the desk from Sanetoshi in his exam room, staring blankly at the CT scan of her own body. She didn't know much about anatomy, but she could see all of her body fat, muscles, and internal organs— the things keeping her alive and moving on a daily basis.

"Stunning, isn't it?" Sanetoshi asked, noticing the direction of her gaze and smiling faintly. Her expression was so serious, one would think she was trying to search her soul through the X-ray images. "Now, allow me to tell you a love story."

The chair creaked as he rose to his feet. Then he pulled down all the images from the film viewer.

"You take one step forward, he takes one step back. You take one step back, he takes one step forward. It was all going so well, but then one day he became distant, and now he's gone. So, what would you do in that situation?"

Stunned by the sudden question, Himari paused just long enough to take a breath.

"If it were me, I wouldn't chase him," she answered.

She was wearing a white angora sweater and a white knee-length gathered skirt over thick wine-colored wool leggings and her usual cowgirl boots.

"Why not?"

Sanetoshi stood in the middle of the large clock projected on the wall. Here in the dimly lit exam room, his lab coat and starched button-down were tinged sky-blue. His charcoal gray pants and black shoes blended in with the shadows, while his cosmic eyes and long, pale rainbow hair seemed to glow by contrast.

"It seems like it'd be exhausting."

"Sure, that's a perfectly valid opinion to have. So you're saying you only want to be chased, never the other way around." He smiled, raising his eyebrows.

"What's that supposed to mean?" She tilted her head slightly as she looked at him. His eyes were speckled with stars, but no amount of gazing into them helped her get a read on him.

"Well, if neither of you chases the other, you're essentially telling each other that you refuse to make the first move."

"What's so bad about that?" Himari asked, staring at the floor.

"No romance will ever come of it," Sanetoshi declared offhandedly.

"So what? I don't need romance," she shot back flatly. But as soon as the words left her lips, terror set in. It felt like she could hear love slowly infecting her heart like a virus.

From Himari's point of view, it would be far too greedy to try to fall in love with someone when she was so deeply lacking as a person. That greed, in turn, would cause problems for Kanba and Shoma. She already required a ton of support, and a tremendous amount of sacrifice, just to make it through each day; she couldn't possibly ask for more. Thus, she had given up on romance...but she still spent every day pining.

"I see." Sanetoshi quietly returned to his chair and crossed his legs. "So you reject romance."

The room fell silent. Himari snuck a glance at him, then hesitantly began to speak.

"Hypothetically speaking..."

I'm just curious, that's all, she reassured herself.

"Yes?"

"If the other person starts to pull away from me, am I *supposed* to chase them? And that's how romance starts?"

"Sometimes, yes," he answered slowly.

"Are you sure? Because if they're just going to keep running away the whole time, I can't imagine my efforts would...bear fruit."

She couldn't explain why, but she got the sense that those who ran would simply keep running forever. There was really no point in chasing them—they would fade into the distance until eventually they vanished from sight altogether. And if no amount of chasing would bring them back, then that energy was better off conserved. Both sides of this hypothetical romance were better off staying right where they were and keeping their "fruit" to themselves.

"A keen observation. Yes, the one who runs will never give anything to the one who chases. They don't want the game to be too easy, after all. They want you to keep chasing," Sanetoshi smirked.

"That's not very nice."

Was romance really just a game? Himari didn't think so at all, but at the same time, she had never consciously experienced it for herself, so she didn't have any ground to stand on in this debate. After all, she was only now starting to recognize that sort of love.

"When it comes down to it, you want the fruit. It's not enough *just* to kiss them, right?" The chair creaked as he rose to his feet. Then he leaned right into Himari's face, peering into her big, round eyes from above.

"Well, I only have so many kisses to give. So if there's no fruit behind it, I'm going to end up empty," she sighed. Her gaze was firm as she stared back at him, but her voice was several degrees more feeble.

"Is there something wrong with being empty?" he whispered, leaning closer. His glowing hair tickled her pale cheek.

"When something's empty, it gets thrown away," she explained, looking up at him.

"So what if you get thrown away? You can strike back with a hundred more kisses."

Slowly, his lips drew close to hers.

"No, I can't. If I get thrown away, my heart will turn to ice, and I'll suffocate," she replied unflinchingly.

"Then just be careful not to kiss quite that much," Sanetoshi grinned, enjoying her defiant stubbornness.

"That's cheating." Himari's long lashes trembled, sparkling like they were damp.

"Nothing wrong with cheating if it means you can kiss."

He straightened up, running a hand through his hair. Meanwhile, she stared at the floor in contemplation. As he gazed at her, he rubbed his thumb over his lower lip. Personally, he didn't care one whit about kissing, or whether it counted as cheating. All that mattered to him was acquiring that fruit, regardless of the means.

"If you're going to turn to ice either way, you might as well do something to deserve it, don't you think? It'd be far more fun to be punished for an avalanche of kisses."

This was another source of energy for him: whether or not something was *fun*.

"Then what am I supposed to do?"

"In summary, follow your heart. I should think kissing itself is its own kind of fruit."

"But then why...?" Why were humans programmed to fall in love? If it was only about kissing, then no one would ever get their heart broken.

Himari thought about last night—about what she remembered and the truth therein. In that memory, she accepted an apple; was that the fruit of romance? Was that the source of the pain she felt in her chest?

There was a voice in her head, telling her Shoma was her soul mate. If what she felt was in fact true love, then chasing it would only bring pain to her and everyone around her. Their family would surely split apart, and chances were good it would spark a domino effect of other, more unpleasant memories rising to the forefront of her mind. If so, she would regret ever falling in love. In fact, she might even feel guilty for remembering who her soul mate truly was.

"Dr. Sanetoshi, why did you want to talk to me about love? Are *you* in love?"

He smiled softly. "Why, yes. And it makes every moment simply *stunning.*"

Sanetoshi couldn't afford to let his guard down for even an instant. After all, his sneaky little lover, Momoka, was surely watching this unfold just as he was—watching this young girl stare down at her hands with the countenance of a grown woman. And Sanetoshi was planning to keep showering his lover in a hailstorm of kisses without ever turning to ice. But his kisses weren't guaranteed to be soft and sweet. At times they could sizzle and burn with the intensity of a raging fire.

At the dumpsters out behind the school building, a handful of students, including me and Yamashita, were tasked with sorting the trash into two large bags: burnable and nonburnable.

"Burnable...nonburnable...burnable...nonburnable... Wait, what about this one? Uhhh...I guess it's nonburnable," Yamashita sighed lazily as he used his trash-picking tongs to toss an empty can into the bag. "Ugh, this sucks... Punished with *chores*? What are we, five?"

I was so distracted thinking about my family situation, I was practically sorting on autopilot. Frankly, it was highly inefficient to make us sort the trash after lumping it all together to begin with. With a building of this size, they should have known just how much waste was produced on a daily basis. They'd save a ton of time if they set up two different trash cans in each location and taught the students to sort their trash into the correct can. Heck, even our house had two different trash cans for that reason. But I couldn't actually point this out or else everyone would call me a househusband.

"We were just minding our business, but because we happened to be in the wrong place at the wrong time, it turned into some crap about 'collective responsibility' or whatever. Why should *we* have to be punished? It's *their* fault! So stupid. One bad apple spoils the rest of us, I tell ya," Yamashita complained quietly into my ear. Then he paused to crack his neck.

He had a point, though. Kanba and Himari and I had nothing to do with our parents' crimes, so it was completely unfair for any of us to have to pay the price for it. We never *chose* to be related to them, but as a result, we were forced to carry the burden of responsibility for the rest of our lives.

"Oh yeah, that reminds me, Shoma-kun..." Yamashita donned a sinister smirk. "How'd it go with that one girl?"

"What one girl?" I shot him a withering look.

"The cute one! From the onsen! She seemed kinda touchy, but I could go for that."

"Things are...normal, I guess?" I told him, though I didn't actually know what *normal* looked like.

"What do you mean, normal? Don't tell me you're already an item!" he gasped, recoiling melodramatically.

"Wh-what? No! We're not an item!"

Oginome-san was a good friend, but the subject had never come up. Granted, I was done shutting her out of my life, but merely changing my perspective was not enough to change the past. It didn't solve everything.

"Man...I'd love to date a chick from Oukagyoen..."

"I'm telling you, we're not dating! Maybe you'd actually get a girlfriend if you stopped making assumptions all the time!"

I started working faster, but I was in no real rush to leave campus. Although I knew for a fact that Kanba and Himari would both come home in due time, I was terrified at the thought of spending a single minute sitting alone in that empty house, waiting for them. But of course, the task at hand eventually came to an end. Naturally, Yamashita was totally jealous that I finished ahead of him. After I managed to calm him down, I slung my book bag over my shoulder, tied my blue-and-beige tartan scarf around my neck, and trudged off in the direction of the school gates.

For some reason, my brain recalled the conversation I had with Kanba about why Yamashita could never get a girlfriend. Annoying, no filter, unfunny... Honestly, the latter two were basically the same thing as annoying...

"Shoma-kun!" Oginome-san called, leaning against the wall just outside the gates, wearing a light school-issued jacket. I forced a smile.

"Oh, hey, Oginome-san. Were you waiting for me? You could have sent me an email, you know."

"I just showed up on a whim, that's all. Glad I could see you," she replied, looking into my eyes and smiling—a pure, genuine smile that caught me by surprise. She saw my expression shift. "What's wrong?" she asked, frowning slightly.

I looked into her big, round eyes, and for the first time in my life, I felt a strong urge to talk about myself. I wanted her to understand me.

Oginome-san never once tried to force anything out of me. As our bodies swayed with the train's motions, I gazed out at the darkness beyond the window and thought back to that dream I once had about an endless dark railroad and a train that never stopped—or rather, *couldn't* stop. Not yet.

"The punishment was meant for me," I explained slowly. "If the Takakura family deserves punishment, then it should be dealt to me alone."

"What do you mean?" Furrowing her brow, Oginome-san looked at me in concern.

"I'll never forgive my parents. Their actions killed countless people, and your sister was one of their..."

Victims. But I couldn't bring myself to say the word. Faltering, I looked down at my feet, where Penguin No. 2 sat, looking back at me.

"It's not your fault, Shoma-kun," she told me gently. Slowly, I shook my head.

"The crimes of the Takakura family are my crimes and no one else's."

"Why do you say that?"

I broke eye contact with No. 2.

"*I* chose Himari to be part of my family. *I* made her a Takakura. *I* dragged her into this mess."

I had tried my hardest to forget this truth, and in fact, it felt like I had succeeded. I had erased the memory from my past.

As I recounted my story, Oginome-san looked at me and listened in perfect silence.

Eight winters ago, I was sitting in a room in a high-rise condo building—the office where my father worked. Reason being, my parents were both very busy, so they couldn't leave me at home or else I'd be on my own for hours and hours. Thus, my father always brought me here to the office. But even then, I was still on my own.

They called it "the office," but looking back, it was just a room in a condo that my parents' organization designated as their headquarters. My father stood in the center of a big group of grown-ups, all of them wearing the same work uniform, and as he gave his long speeches reminiscent of a school assembly, I sat there watching, bored to tears.

"On that day, a tiny fragment of this corrupted world was purified by our holy fire. But our mission has not yet been achieved. Society calls us criminals, and on that day, many of our comrades were unjustly taken prisoner. But that is not enough to extinguish the flames of the torch we carry in our hearts. Now is the time to lie low; the name change was necessary just to shake off those fascist pigs. Instead, we must solemnly prepare for the next Day of Reckoning. Peace!"

My father held his hand up high in a peace sign, and his audience followed suit. It was a popular gesture here at my father's workplace, but I wasn't sure what exactly it meant. All I knew was that it looked like "scissors" from rock-paper-scissors. Or was it like "V for Victory"?

Here at the office, I would occasionally meet other kids around the same age as me. There were two siblings—a boy and a girl, both with narrow eyes and fancy clothes, who were much better behaved than I was. They always paid attention to the speeches.

As I retrieved my down jacket from the chair in the corner and wrapped myself up in my scarf, the girl called out to me: "You there! Where are you going?"

Her hair was curly, and her voice carried very well.

"Aren't you going to listen to the speeches?!" she continued in an accusatory tone, after I failed to answer her first question.

"He's probably bored," her brother shrugged, tossing a bright red apple back and forth between his hands.

"But the next speech is even more important! Our father will be speaking!" the girl protested. Her brother, however, merely shot me a glance without saying anything.

I didn't say a word to him, either. Instead, I stepped into my sneakers, opened the door, and dashed out of the office. The sharp chill made me flinch.

Truth be told, I was sick to death of sitting around while my father did his work. I tucked one of the apples from the office into my jacket pocket, but I didn't particularly like apples to begin with. I scanned the quiet building's square-shaped hallway, then started walking. A few steps later, I pulled the apple out of my pocket. In this foggy white world, it gleamed like a ruby.

Leaning against the railing, I rolled the apple around on my palm as I peered down into the courtyard, square-shaped and covered in dead grass. Up above, I could see an equally square-shaped piece of the winter sky. And on the floor below mine, I could see a small figure crouched in one corner.

Pushing the apple back into my pocket, I casually descended the staircase, hoping I found someone I could play with. But when I got a good look at the girl sitting against the railing, I started to have second thoughts. She had long hair, and despite the weather, she was only wearing a wool jersey dress and a pair of plain boat shoes with no socks. Both the dress and the shoes were grimy with dirt, and the girl in question seemed like she was in a daze. In one hand, she clutched the paw of a large peach-pink teddy bear.

"Hey, do you live here?"

I didn't strike up a conversation *purely* out of boredom; no, I was a tiny bit worried about her, too. She looked at me with big, round eyes, her gaze tinged with suspicion.

"What are you up to?"

At the very least, she didn't look like she was having fun playing by herself. If she was lost, I figured I could get my father to help.

"...I'm waiting for Mama," she muttered after a long moment.

"How long have you been waiting?" Maybe she really was lost.

"The whole time," she said in a monotone voice.

"And how long is that?"

Minutes? Hours? Based on her dirty clothes, I suspected it was more like days or weeks. The thought frightened me a bit.

"I don't know." She blinked at me in confusion.

"Wanna play?"

She shook her head. "I have to wait for Mama." But she clearly looked miserable.

"Aren't you cold?"

Even in my down jacket, I could feel the stinging chill against my cheeks and through the gaps in my pants. She fell silent and stared at the ground, exhaling white fog. Of *course* she was cold. So I took off my bright blue-and-yellow striped scarf, crouched down, and wrapped it around her neck instead. "You can borrow this."

The girl looked at me in shock. She didn't say a word, but she reached up and touched the fabric of the scarf, her eyes as round as saucers.

"Want my apple?" I sat down next to her and pulled the fruit out of my pocket.

"No. Mama said not to take food from strangers."

Admittedly I, too, was taught not to take things from strangers or go places with them, but I was pretty sure those rules only applied to *grown-up* strangers. Looking back, I could see how kid-me wouldn't have been too worried about other kids...but at the same time, strangers were still strangers, regardless of age.

"Say, do you know the story of the first man and woman on Earth?" I asked, unable to bear the continued silence.

"Nope," she answered indifferently.

I only recently learned this story myself. "They say they shared the fruit of fate."

"In my life, there's no such thing as fruit."

As she spoke, she rose to her feet, pulled off the scarf, and thrust it back at me. Then she pulled her teddy bear into her arms and took off like a gust of wind, her long hair trailing behind her as she ran. As for me, I stood there, the wrapped-up scarf in one hand and the apple in the other, alone and bored once again.

The next time I came to the condo building, I snuck two chocolate treats into the pocket of my down jacket. This time I was purposely going to search for the girl.

"What are you up to?"

I found her in the basement, curled up next to the trash dump reserved for tenants. She was wearing the exact same clothes as last time, and she looked like she was freezing.

"I found a cat," she said in a tiny voice, looking at me in alarm.

"Is it yours?" I asked, walking over to her. The girl shook her head.

She was huddled over a small box. Inside, a tiny tabby kitten shivered helplessly.

"What's it doing here?"

"Nobody wanted it," she replied in a scarcely audible voice.

"But it's so cute! C'mere, kitty." I crouched down and offered it my hand. It recoiled in fear and scurried away to the far corner of the box.

"I bet it was loved at first. But then it used up all its loveable-ness and got thrown away," the girl explained. Startled, I looked at her face in profile...but her long hair concealed everything except her eyelashes and the tip of her nose.

"Oh, I know. Want me to go get some milk?" I asked. I was trying to help the kitten—or at least, that was my intention.

"Stop. You can't keep it, right?"

"Well...no..." I was ashamed of myself for even *thinking* of such a childish, irresponsible suggestion.

"If you aren't chosen, then you're discarded and left to die." She was so quiet and still, I couldn't tell whether she was sad or not.

Unloved, discarded, left behind to die. She said she was waiting for her mother, but what did she really mean by that? Was she truly "waiting for her mother" all alone in a condo building, with only a dirty dress to her name?

"Well, it's not dead yet," I muttered.

Once again, she looked at me in surprise. She also seemed a tiny bit angry. But though the kitten could have evaded her detection if it really wanted to, it instead revealed itself to her. And now here it was, living and breathing right in front of us.

Using a cardboard box and some towels I found in the trash, I built a new house for the kitten out behind the building—one with a roof and everything. In place of a bed, I rolled up my scarf like a little nest. Timidly, the kitten wandered in and curled up into a little ball. Then I brought some of the milk from the office fridge on a saucer, which the girl and I presented to the kitten.

"Can it drink cow's milk?" she asked anxiously.

"It's gotta be really hungry," I replied as I set the saucer in front of the box.

Together, we crouched down and peered at the kitten. Cautiously, it approached the saucer, gave it a sniff, then started lapping at the milk with its little tongue.

"It's drinking it!"

"Let's look after it until we can find it a new owner. I promise, I'll ask around."

Neither of us could keep the kitten, but I refused to abandon it. So the only option left was to find someone who could take over for us. That way it wouldn't be cruel to prolong its life.

"Okay."

Then, for the first time, the girl's expression softened a tiny bit. It warmed my heart.

As we ate the chocolate treats I'd pulled from my pocket, we watched over the now-satiated kitten as it toddled back to the stripey scarf to take a nap.

"It's so cute," I commented. The girl nodded quietly. And as the chocolate melted on her tongue, her lips curled into a tiny smile.

From then on, I would make regular visits to the condo building to see the girl and the cat, smuggling snacks in my pockets each time. Playing with them was the highlight of my day. Neither of us knew how to handle a cat, so we couldn't pet it much at first, but gradually it began to trust us, and eventually we were graciously allowed to run our hands down its back.

"It's so soft." The girl never talked much, but over time her face became more and more expressive. "Kittens are really warm, huh?"

"Hey, guess what? I brought some ribbons we can tie around its neck. Just some stuff I found at home."

In the kitchen drawer, I discovered some old ribbons that were once used to wrap parcels, so I stuffed a few into my pocket. One of them was wine red with gold lettering, originally from a bakery box. There were also pink and blue ones from past birthday and Christmas gifts.

"They're pretty," the girl murmured quietly, entranced.

"Which one is the best?"

I lined them up for her to see. She didn't answer, but her eyes were fixed on the pink ribbon—a thin and glossy one.

"Do you like pink?"

She nodded slightly.

With the pink ribbon newly tied around its neck, the kitten seemed annoyed at first, but slowly adapted to it. Then I introduced it to the canned food I bought, and before long, it would trot over to us the moment we arrived, purring up a storm.

"I hope we can find someone who can give it a home," the girl muttered, gently cradling the small, warm kitten. Compared to when I first met her, she slowly started to change into a different girl—a sweet, caring girl with an adorable smile and a passion for all things cute. Her complexion looked pale, exacerbated by her dark dress plus the winter air, but her big, round eyes gleamed like precious gems.

"I've been asking around at school, but I haven't found anyone yet," I admitted, feeling guilty.

"Oh..."

The girl was definitely younger than me, but there were times that she seemed abnormally calm, or maybe detached, like she'd given up on the whole world. Most likely it had something to do with her mother, who never seemed to show up. But I was just a kid—I couldn't pry about her home life. It would be no different from feeding a cat I couldn't keep. After all, a thoughtless, power-less *child* couldn't possibly be of any help. I was just a nobody.

Our little cardboard house was located right behind the condo building. This was the best spot we could think of to keep it hidden. We didn't care if we got dirty—we would flop down and put our heads in the box, letting the kitten sniff at our faces and curl up on our chests.

"What should we name it?"

Randomly, it occurred to me that we only ever referred to it as "Meow meow" or "Pss pss pss" or "Kitty." Even if we were only fostering it temporarily, it still deserved a temporary nickname.

"You want to name it?" The girl contemplated this as she played with the kitten using the green foxtail I'd plucked from the ground. Then she set the toy down and gently scooped up the feisty little kitten. "Well, it's warm like the sun, and it smells like sunshine." She nuzzled her face against its fur.

Then, at last, I managed to ask the critical question: "What's *your* name, anyway?"

"Himari. It means *sunny spot*," she explained with a bashful smile.

"Wow, that's a pretty name. Okay then, let's give the kitten a matching nickname! How about Sunshine? Hmm...maybe not..." I grimaced at my own lack of naming sense.

"San-chan."

Her voice was so quiet, I nearly missed it.

"San-chan? Oh, I get it. *Sun*, the English word. Yeah, I like it!"

As I spoke, I reached out and stroked San-chan's little head as Himari cradled it in her arms. It closed its eyes contentedly.

Himari looked up at me and beamed, blushing. Then she looked down at the kitten nodding off to sleep against her chest and whispered, "San-chan..."

It was a day like any other. Once again, Himari and I traveled to the condo building to see San-chan. The snow that fell that morning gave the old, familiar city a fresh coat of white paint, absorbing all noise as it piled up.

Had Himari caught the flu? Was she still waiting outside for her mother, even when it was snowing? Sure, maybe I couldn't help her family situation, but she was always so pale and thin and cold... Honestly, I worried about her more than I worried about the cat. But something told me that if I pried for details, I would never see her again.

I was just a kid.

In the corner of the square-shaped hallway, Himari sat clinging to the railing.

"Himari-chan!"

She was looking up at the sky, probably watching the snow fall. Then she whirled around excitedly, still wearing the same dingy dress. Together, we walked to San-chan's house, just like always.

A small amount of snow had piled on the roof of the cardboard box, and the scarf nest was empty—no sign of the kitten. We searched around as best we could, but failed to find San-chan.

"Everything's all wet," Himari frowned, touching the scarf.

"Maybe it tried to find someplace warmer."

The first place we thought of was the trash dump area in the basement of the building where Himari first found San-chan. There were plenty of places to hide there, and it was bound to be a little warmer indoors... We exchanged a glance, then headed to the basement. But when we arrived, the garbage collection truck was already revving up its engine.

"No!"

San-chan's tiny box disappeared behind the rotating plate. The trash dump area was now completely empty. Meanwhile, I thought back to what I learned in school about garbage collection. When you pressed the switch, the rotating plate compressed the trash deep into the truck. Then it was taken to a waste incineration plant...

"Wait!"

Hastily, I ran after the truck. It drove out onto the snowy street and sped away.

"WAIT!"

Breathing in the icy air made my chest sting. As I ran at full speed, the falling snow flew into my face, melting into cold water. Wiping the snow from my eyelashes with one hand, I kept on running. Here in the silent city, all I could hear was the rumble of the truck's engine and my own labored breathing.

Then, eventually, the truck disappeared into the white, foggy distance. Coughing and wheezing, I doubled over, clutching my knees as I tried to catch my breath. At my feet, the garbage truck left behind a long trail of dark tire tracks.

When I returned to the condo building, I found Himari standing by the entrance to the basement parking lot, staring at the ground.

"I'm sorry."

Tears filled my eyes. I was the one who suggested we look after the cat in the first place, and I was the one who failed to find a forever home for it. Maybe I didn't try hard enough. Maybe part of me just wanted to keep raising it with Himari.

"It's not your fault, Sho-chan," she said quietly. It was freezing cold, and yet she seemingly forgot to shiver. "San-chan just wasn't chosen."

"Huh?"

When she looked up at me, the expression on her face reminded me of the day we first met—neither happy nor sad. And yet, nevertheless, she was crying. I wanted to reassure her... to tell her not to cry...but I couldn't. In the end, we failed to save San-chan.

"In this world, either you're chosen or you're not. And if you're left behind, you die," Himari explained in a hoarse, watery voice that left her lips in a white fog.

And after that day, I never saw Himari at the condo building again.

I searched the whole place from top to bottom. After all, it was possible the kitten was still around, just hiding somewhere, or maybe someone adopted it. And there was something I wanted to tell Himari, even if it was really only a pathetic platitude: *No matter what happened to San-chan in the end, I don't regret taking care of it with you. Saying goodbye hurts, but that doesn't mean it was all a waste of time.*

Unfortunately, Himari was nowhere to be found. Alone, I decided to go ahead and bring the cardboard house back to the trash dump. But when I peered inside, I found a little white piece of paper folded up in the towels. I opened it to find a letter from Himari addressed to me.

"Hey, Dad? What's the 'Child Broiler'?" I asked my father as he gazed out at the snowy scenery through the office window. He looked over his shoulder at me in alarm. "Well?" I pressed.

"It's a place where children are sent when they're forsaken by society. We can't do anything about it, and we can't save them. It's a rusty, closed-off place," my father explained in a low, quiet, yet somewhat pained voice.

"What happens to the kids who go there?"

"They become invisible."

"What do you mean?"

"They never amount to anything."

Based on his tone and expression, I could tell that he was dancing around the crux of the issue. Probably because I was just a kid.

"So they die?" In my pocket, I squeezed the letter from Himari. "How come?"

My father shifted his gaze back to the window. "Right this moment, there are countless children turning invisible as we speak, and this corrupted world continues to turn a blind eye to it. That is why we must purify the world and eradicate all corruption."

But I wasn't listening. The next thing I knew, I broke into a run.

Himari's letter was poorly written and rife with spelling errors, and part of it was wet from melted snow. But to me, those wet spots looked like tears.

Dear Sho-chan,

Goodbye, and thank you for everything. I'm going to the Child Broiler.

It really meant a lot to me the first time you reached out to me. My mama never came back for me, so I decided to wait for you instead. Waiting for you was a lot easier, and I was never lonely.

I liked being a family with you and San-chan, so I'm going to take your scarf as a memento. No matter what happens, I'll never forget you. Our memories together are a precious treasure to me. That's why I'm not scared anymore. Even if I turn invisible, nobody can erase my memories, not even if I burn up in the fireplace like a tin soldier. I'm just happy there's someone in the world who knows I existed.

The truth is, I do know the story of the first man and woman who lived on Earth. They were punished, and being alive was the punishment. But I was willing to be punished if it meant I could stay with you, Sho-chan. That's why I wanted someone to choose me.

I didn't know what the Child Broiler was, or where it was located, or how big of a deal it was to go there. It didn't feel like a real place to me. But Himari was going there, and she was going to disappear without ever amounting to anything. I would never see her again.

I couldn't really picture someone I knew dying. I wouldn't be able to talk to her anymore, and I'd only just gotten her to smile, but now I'd never see her face again, either. Her long hair and pale skin would disappear, and the image of her shivering in the cold would be lost to the world around me, and the thought was painful.

As I ran through the darkness, snow slid into my sneakers and turned my socks into a sloshy mess. My legs were both frozen to the core, and as I ran, the chill turned to pain until eventually I went numb altogether. They were like two columns of ice, carrying me forward as fast as I could go to a destination I hadn't yet specified.

Himari thought of me as her family, and I wanted to save her. I didn't care about the "corruption of the world." I was just desperate to get her back.

Together, the two of us shared many things—the sweet taste of candy, the chill of snow, the thrill of snowball fights, the pain of losing San-chan—but there were still many more ahead. I didn't treat her like family so she would give up on living; I wanted her to realize that there were people in the world who cared about her and wanted to help. And I was going to make her see that—for her own sake, for San-chan's, and for mine.

With my legs bogged down in the snow, I felt as though I was gliding along with the winter wind. In that moment, I was sure I would find Himari, no matter where she went. That was what I decided the moment I grabbed the door handle there in the middle of the blizzard. I was going to choose Himari—I *needed* to.

I couldn't really tell what color or shape or size the door was, and it felt like the handle might fly off in the wind if I didn't hold on tight. But with all my strength, I forced it open little by little, making it creak in protest. Inside, I could hear the whirr of a large, active machine.

"Himari-chan!"

It was a vast, empty space, and somehow it felt even colder inside. There was no wind, and yet the air seemed to sting my face. I could see some big, rusty fans spinning their blades, and a large group of children sat on the ground, packed in tightly, all of them with their knees tucked up to their chins.

"Himari-chan, where are you?!"

Without hesitation, I ran inside. The ice-cold air engulfed me, and as I shouted for Himari, every subsequent breath I took made me wheeze. Chunks of ice fell from the endlessly tall ceiling, impeding my path. None of the kids seemed to care that I was looking for someone; they all stared blankly at the ground. None of them looked especially cold, either—just depressed and defeated.

I snaked my way through the crowd, searching for Himari. The ice rained on me mercilessly, slashing at my face, my hands—any inch of exposed skin. Meanwhile, the temperature continued to plummet. At this rate, my whole body would freeze solid.

"Himari-chan!"

Out of the corner of my eye, I spotted a familiar blue-and-yellow striped scarf, standing out in sharp relief against the monochrome like the beacon of a lighthouse. As I ran toward it, the dark floor moved like a conveyor belt, carrying Himari away as she lay down with her eyes closed, clasping her hands at her chest.

"Wait!" I ran up and touched her pale cheek. She was *startlingly* cold. "Himari-chan! *Himari!*"

Again and again, I called her name, pressing both palms to her cheeks to keep her warm. And when I saw my scarf wrapped tightly around her neck, I fought back tears.

"Himari, it's me. Let's go home."

I huddled over her, shielding her face from the falling ice chunks. As I kept calling for her and blocking the ice with my body, her frozen face regained a tiny bit of its color. When I touched her ashen forehead, I found it faintly warm. All at once, the harsh blizzard seemed to melt into peaceful silence.

"Himari."

Her long lashes fluttered, and she slowly opened her big, round eyes.

"Aah..."

Her cry was high-pitched and wispy, like a baby bird's. As she stared at me in a daze, I sat back and smiled at her. Then I pulled out the apple I had stowed away in my jacket pocket and offered it to her.

"Let's share the fruit of fate," I choked.

There were so many other, better things I could have said instead, like "Now you'll never have to wait around by yourself ever again" or "Let's go someplace warmer." But I didn't care about anything else—I was just happy she was safe.

"Thank you for choosing me."

Smiling, Himari took the apple of life and punishment from my hand. It gleamed scarlet, lighting up our faces like a tiny burning sun. Then I grabbed her hand, and from that day forward, she became part of my family.

Kanba wouldn't join until a short while later.

At a little ramen shop shrouded in the darkness of dusk, Kanba sat at the bright red counter, hunched over with his hands in the pockets of his black military jacket, trying to stave off the cold. Kenzan and Chiemi sat beside him, staring down at themselves quietly. Then, with a hard look on his face, Kenzan straightened his posture.

"Right this very moment, there are countless children turning invisible as we speak. We cannot allow this corrupted world to turn a blind eye to it any longer! That is why we must bring about the Day of Reckoning and purify the world!"

Chiemi gazed at her husband, taking in every word.

"Himari needs money for her medical expenses, and as far as I know, I'm the only one who can save her," Kanba muttered, his low voice contrasting starkly with his father's gravitas. "But nothing's *working*! No matter how much money I scrape together, Himari's disease refuses to be cured!"

"We live in a corrupt society, restricted by rules put in place by the greedy," Kenzan replied, placing a reassuring hand on Kanba's shoulder.

"Yeah...it's society's fault..." With his cold, pink hands, Kanba clutched at his hair. "Or have I been going about it the wrong way?"

"You've done nothing wrong, Kanba. I can tell you're working as hard as you can to protect the family," Chiemi replied with a smile.

"Please, son. Save Himari from this corrupted world."

"You're the only one who can, sweetheart."

Silently, Kanba looked up.

"I'm proud to have brought you into the Takakura family," Kenzan declared, exchanging a glance with Chiemi. With a smile, she gently stroked Kanba's soft, short, messy hair.

"You, Shoma, and Himari—the three of you are our precious children. And our precious future."

Himari stood in the kitchen with Penguin No. 3, getting dinner ready for when her brothers came home. With her long hair tied in pigtails, she watched over her simmering pot with a contented smile.

"Good thing we had all the ingredients to make cream stew. It's cold out there."

Then No. 3 attempted to nibble at the roux brick.

"Stop that, San-chan! It's not ready yet!"

Himari snatched the rectangular brick, reminiscent of a bar of white chocolate, out of the penguin's little flippers. Then she narrowed her eyes and gave her best evil laugh.

"The waters are boiling, just as planned. Now, let us add the magic powder imported from a distant land... Yes, it shall bubble like white-hot lava!"

As she broke off pieces of the roux brick and slowly added them to the pot, she giggled at her own silly performance.

"I hope Sho-chan and Kan-chan get home soon," she sighed, stirring the pot with a ladle. The roux gradually melted, and a gentle scent rose up. "Say, San-chan, wanna be my taste-tester?"

No. 3 jumped up excitedly. With a smile, Himari poured a bit of the stew onto a saucer, crouched down, and handed it to the penguin.

"Remember, it's hot, so be careful."

No. 3 obediently blew the steam from the liquid, then downed it with such force, it nearly swallowed the whole saucer.

"What do you think? Is it good?"

The penguin blushed happily. Himari beamed back.

"I'm gonna add some salt and pepper and give it a little more time to simmer, and then it'll be ready!" She scooped No. 3 into her arms and gave it a nuzzle. "There's lots and lots, so have as much as you want, okay?"

Not to suggest that she wasn't a tiny bit worried, but right now, all she could do was wait for her family to come home. It felt like the right thing to do.

"I wonder if they'll notice I added more embroidery to the curtains."

Three new stars now were sewn into the fabric near the top. As she stood on the sofa, swiftly working her needle in and out, it occurred to her just how important it was to stay focused at a time like this.

Over the course of her life spent in and out of hospitals, there were many times that she found herself paralyzed from over-thinking. In those cases, the most effective options were either to go to sleep or to concentrate on some other task. This applied to anything from contemplating her own mortality to thinking about romance or the future.

To Himari, family was very important. To that end, there were times when she needed to turn her brain off and stop thinking altogether.

PENGUINDRUM

CHAPTER 03 ··· →

ON THE WAY HOME FROM SCHOOL, Ringo boarded the subway train with Yukina and Mari. They chatted for a while, and then it was time for Mari to deboard, followed by Yukina. Then the train passed Ringo's station, too.

For a while now, Ringo had gotten into the habit of going to hang out at the Takakura house. Well, perhaps "hang out" wasn't the right way to put it—she was checking up on them. Sometimes she made plans with Himari, while other times she met up with Shoma. But in the end, she always checked in with all three siblings.

Granted, she was still coming to terms with everything she'd learned about their history. But in the meantime, she spent her days worrying endlessly about whether they were still functioning as a family...and whether anyone was giving them any trouble.

Yukina and Mari often teased her about "finally finding a boyfriend," but she and Shoma were *not* dating—for now, at least.

In a way, he felt more like a brother or some other relative...not that she believed she could insert herself into the ironclad bond between the three Takakura siblings, of course. But if possible, she wanted to build a good, strong connection with the first person she ever truly loved.

Tabuki Keiju was still nowhere to be found. Ringo was no longer interested in chasing after him, but she kept thinking back to the look in his eyes the last time she saw him. Those were the eyes of a kind, responsible man—the same Tabuki she had previously convinced herself she was in love with.

Had she become a better person? Even if she couldn't be Momoka, could she still help Shoma? Was she useful to him? Was she needed?

Having deboarded at Ogikubo Station, she headed up the stairs. The wind blew up from below, rustling her hair. Her school-issued balmacaan coat was far too thin for this weather, and her bare neck was freezing.

"Oginome Ringo-san, I presume?"

Just then, she was accosted by a short man with a wan complexion who reeked of cigarette smoke. Suspicious, she stayed quiet.

"Allow me to identify myself." He pulled a business card with bent corners out of his pocket and offered it to her.

"A journalist?"

Positioned over his name was the logo of a weekly tabloid that published all sorts of entertainment articles, including erotic model shoots. Ringo had seen this magazine at the convenience store, but she'd never read one. Its content wasn't always strictly factual.

"We're looking to interview the family members of those lost in the bombing. Now, we've heard it told that a group of children are living in the house of suspect Takakura Kenzan, pretending to be siblings. What do you think of this? Your older sister was killed in that incident, correct?"

Maybe he thought his smile was reassuring, but to Ringo, it was stiff, unnatural, and downright goosebump-inducing.

"Don't write about things you know nothing about!" she shot back, glaring.

"It's the truth, isn't it? The world has a right to know. This is what it means to get justice," the journalist replied robotically.

Ringo ignored him and stormed off into the shopping district. The journalist watched her go with a faint smile on his face, then turned and left.

"God, that journalist pissed me off! Next time I see him, he's getting a knuckle sandwich! You better be on the lookout for him, Himari-chan!" Ringo raged melodramatically, then took a sip of the hot cocoa Himari made for her. "Agh! Hot!"

"I will." As her expression clouded over, Himari transferred her cookies (freshly baked following Ringo's recipe) onto a plate.

"Seriously, I mean it. Okay, end of conversation!" Pouting, Ringo let out a sigh and looked over at Himari as she continued to avert her gaze. "I'm sorry... I know you went to all the trouble of making cookies for me..."

"It's okay."

Himari followed Ringo's recipe by herself once before, but at some point she must have put in the wrong amount of something, because they came out rock-hard. Shoma and Kanba still ate them, claiming they were "tasty in their own way" and "might make our teeth stronger." But this time they came out perfectly—crispy, crunchy, and golden brown, with a light melt-in-your-mouth sweetness, just like the recipe intended.

"So...I guess you found out that the three of us aren't really siblings, huh?"

Now that she remembered, she wasn't really planning to keep it a secret from Ringo, but she wasn't sure she was emotionally ready to find out how her friend felt about the special circumstances of the Takakura household.

"Yeah, Shoma-kun told me a little while back," Ringo answered, feeling a bit guilty.

"Oh, so Sho-chan told you."

For the briefest of moments, resentment flared up inside Himari at the thought that Shoma had snuck off to have some secret conversation with Ringo. As with the night the four of them ate sukiyaki together, she felt vaguely left out.

"I'm sorry," Ringo apologized on reflex, though she hadn't done anything wrong.

"No, it's okay—I wanted you to know about it. It sucks having to lie all the time."

It was the honest truth. Himari was happy to share her secrets with a friend as dear as Ringo... In that moment, looking down at her violet cable knit sweater dress, her slender legs looked small and childish.

"Well, have a cookie," she said at last, forcing the words out as she looked up at Ringo, who gazed back anxiously. "I think they turned out good this time."

"Okay!" Ringo grabbed a little round cookie and popped it into her mouth.

"How is it?" Himari asked.

"It's good!" Ringo beamed.

Himari smiled back, then ate one herself. "What a relief."

They all cared about each other, and they were all working hard to do right by each other. Maybe Shoma was having a really hard time not being able to talk to Kanba, since he was constantly busy with work, and maybe he didn't want to bother Himari either, since she was so frail. Maybe it was a good thing, then, that Ringo was there for him. Yes, of course. Hadn't the three of them always cared about each other, right from the start?

"See, our house is actually a Mika-chan Dream House," Himari explained calmly.

"What? Mika-chan, like the doll?"

"Uh huh. Remember Mika-chan and her Dream House?"

Himari could still remember the commercial jingle, clear as day. She started to sing it, and before long Ringo joined in. At the end, they both burst out laughing.

"Oh god, that takes me back! Now I remember. I wanted one so bad, but my parents wouldn't buy it for me."

"Same." Nearby, Penguin No. 3 sat on the tatami busily knitting; Himari pulled it into a hug. "Did you know it was Kan-chan and Sho-chan that painted the wall outside?"

"What?"

"Back when Mom and Dad first disappeared, I would cry all day long. With each new day, I was terrified that Kan-chan and Sho-chan would leave me, just like *they* did."

But then Kanba and Shoma started painting the sheet metal siding in a rainbow of different colors. Pink and blue and green and yellow and red and orange... In a blink, Himari watched as the dull, gray house transformed into something bright and beautiful.

When they finished, the two boys thrust out their chests proudly, both of them splattered with drops of paint. Himari promptly stopped crying, instead staring enraptured at the wall that now resembled a Mika-chan Dream House. Whenever their parents returned, she was sure they would be delighted to see it. Afterwards, the boys reached out and stroked her hair with their newly paint-free hands.

"Wow, that's so cool! That wall was one of the first things I noticed about your house. I didn't realize your brothers did it themselves."

"Yup. And they made me a matching Mika-chan bed, too."

"Oh my god, I was *wondering* why it seemed so familiar! It's a Mika-chan Princess Bed!"

Their mother had left an ancient sewing machine behind in one of the rooms. There, they got to work, using tons of old books and fabric to transform Himari's rickety little metal bed frame. Then they added four posts and a canopy, and just like that, it was the Mika-chan Princess Bed she always dreamed of.

Then Himari herself learned to knit and sew. With some assistance, she made little additions, like cushions and shelves. Over time, she collected candles and lamps in the shape of angels and mushrooms, and now it was every girl's fantasy bedroom.

"It really meant a lot to me."

"Aww, they're such good brothers!"

"But then they stepped on my favorite teddy bear and made its stuffing pop out."

Horrified, they hastily comforted a crying Himari, then set about giving the little bear's tummy some much-needed "first aid," inexperienced though they were.

"See this stitching here? It looks like the poor thing had surgery." Himari grabbed the pink pirate teddy bear from her bedroom to show Ringo.

"You're right! Aww, it's so cute. Bad stitch job, though," she laughed.

"Yeah, but that's what makes it so special. I consider it his appendectomy scar."

"I guess those two dorks were bound to screw something up sooner or later."

"It's okay. Mistakes like these are proof that we're a family."

"Awww..." Touched, Ringo ran a finger over the bear's stomach. She didn't notice Himari's expression steadily growing darker once more.

In the end, Himari sent Ringo home with half of the cookies. And after she was gone, Himari stood there in the entryway, staring into space.

Just prior to Ringo's visit, the magazine journalist had already arrived at the Takakura house while Himari was home alone.

"You realize your medical expenses are incredibly costly, right?"

He was a short, stocky man who stank of cigarettes, and this was the first thing he asked her, without even so much as a perfunctory greeting.

"Why would you ask me that?" Himari asked back, without meeting his gaze.

"Because no high schooler could possibly scrape together that kind of cash."

"What are you trying to say?"

Part of her was desperate for Ringo or Shoma or Kanba to come home and rescue her, but another part of her wanted to know the truth. Thus, she didn't send him away.

Kanba never said a word about Sanetoshi's expensive medical treatments beyond a dismissive "Don't worry about it," and somehow, his part-time job seemed to be paying enough to cover them. Even Himari could tell that something was fishy about it.

The journalist pulled a stack of photos out of his jacket pocket and showed them to her. The photos depicted Kanba surrounded by a group of men dressed in black, one of them caught in the process of handing him an envelope.

"We've figured out where your brother's been getting the money. It's a huge scoop." Before Himari could ask who the men in black were, he continued, "These men are part of an organization called KIGA—the remnants of the group behind the bombing. In other words, their dirty money is the only thing keeping you alive."

The group behind the bombing. Himari's vision blurred and dimmed. She sensed that Kanba was making a massive sacrifice on her behalf, but the truth was worse than she ever imagined.

"How do you feel about that? I'd love to know."

"Please leave," she choked. Then she slid the door shut and locked it. "Please leave!"

After that, the journalist didn't knock or call out to her again. Then Himari spotted No. 3 standing around idly in the hall. She scooped it up into her arms, then hurried to the kitchen.

"The cookies will be ready soon, okay?"

Her grip on No. 3 grew tighter and tighter. Meanwhile, it peered up at her curiously as she sternly opened the oven door.

Even after Himari pulled on her soft gauzy nightgown and climbed into bed, sleep eluded her. Shoma gave her a hot water bottle to keep the bed warm; as she rolled it around with her feet, she gazed at Penguin No. 3 already slumbering beside her, its little beak twitching sporadically.

Hours later, after tossing and turning until the bottle's warmth was all but lost, she heard the front door slide open and bolted upright. Someone just left the house. Hastily, she sprang out of bed and donned her robe, her coat, a pair of tights, and a scarf. Then she slid open her bedroom door, and sure enough, one of the futons was empty. Kanba was missing.

Careful not to wake Shoma as he snored soundly, Himari tiptoed over the tatami to the entryway, quietly slipped into her sneakers, and walked outside. There, she roughly ran a hand through her long hair. Then she set off down the street.

Shivering in the cold of night, she glanced around. In the distance, she could see Kanba walking away from her, his black coat sporadically illuminated by each streetlamp as he passed under it. Summoning her resolve, Himari decided to tail him.

If what the journalist told her earlier that day was true, then it was quite possible Kanba was meeting up with someone from KIGA…maybe to get more money for the family. She wasn't really sure what her plan was—should she stop him, or was she only interested in confirming the truth with her own two eyes? And if it did turn out to be true, should she tell Shoma? What would he think?

Kanba seemingly paid no heed to his surroundings. When he arrived at the outskirts of town, he walked into a small ramen shop with no lights on inside. Was *this* their meetup spot? Even after he entered the building, the windows remained dark.

Exhaling into her hands, Himari watched from a distance and waited for someone to come outside. Here in this sleepy residential district, the only lights were those of the streetlamps. Shivering, she crouched down, huddling into herself. She didn't own a cell phone, so she couldn't even check the time. Then

Kanba stepped out of the ramen shop, still alone. Biting back the urge to call for him, Himari watched as he headed back the way he came with a hard look on his face.

If she revealed herself right that moment and asked him to come clean, would he?

She watched him stagger down the street and, after a good ten or twenty seconds of serious contemplation, decided not to reveal herself. He wouldn't be honest with her; he would just get angry that she followed him out here this late at night. Then he'd notice that she was shivering and lend her his coat, and with a smile, he'd tell her there was nothing she needed to worry about—and in so doing, he would willfully distance her from the truth, even though she was practically staring it in the face at this point.

She waited until he vanished from sight, then dashed over to the ramen shop. Holding her breath, she forced open the poorly fitted door. For a moment she was scared that the person inside would hear her, but it quickly became apparent that she needn't have worried.

Not only was there no electricity, but it was increasingly apparent that the place hadn't operated as a restaurant in many years. Everything was covered in a layer of dust, and the corners of the ceiling were dotted with thick spiderwebs. Choking on the stench of mold, she covered her nose and mouth with one hand as she entered.

"Hello...?"

Inside, the cramped interior featured a counter with peeling paint and a handful of stools set in front of it. On the walls hung an outdated calendar with the name of a bar on it, a poster of a bikini-clad woman holding a beer stein, and what was probably once the menu, but was now too burned to be legible.

"Is anyone here?"

Following the footprints in the dust likely left behind by Kanba, Himari moved deeper inside the shop. There, she spotted something shiny on the counter; she reached out and pinched it between her thumb and forefinger, holding it up. It was the ring she always yearned to one day wear—more specifically, it was one of the wedding rings Kenzan and Chiemi wore. No diamonds or gaudy adornments, just thin platinum. She didn't know how her father felt about it, but her mother wore it on her person at all times like a precious keepsake.

"Your ring doesn't have a diamond?" little Himari once asked as she sat on her mother's knee. At the time, her mental image of a wedding ring involved a round brilliant-cut diamond the size of a tangerine.

"Not yet! After you grow up and become an idol, will you buy me one?" her mother asked, smiling.

"Of course!" Himari had replied, as if it was the most obvious choice in the world.

Hesitantly, she peered at the inside of the ring. There, the words "K to C" were engraved in the metal. *From Kenzan to Chiemi.*

"Mom?" she called in a quavering voice. The silence of the room grated on her ears. Then she heard a sound like the snapping of a tree branch. But when she looked in that direction, all at once, her mind went blank. The blood drained from her face. The ring slipped from her fingers and plummeted into the dusty darkness.

She thought she had figured out Kanba's secret, but as it turned out, she didn't know the half of it.

Himari was not looking forward to seeing Natsume Masako again. Just the other day, the girl pointed a gun at her; there was no telling what sort of gutting remarks she might make the next time the two of them came face to face. But Himari couldn't keep hiding behind Kanba forever. She came to the conclusion that she'd never figure out what she truly wanted unless she learned the whole truth. And so, per Masako's instructions conveyed to her over the phone, she didn't tell her brothers where she was headed when she left.

"Did you make this?" Masako asked, eyebrows raised, as she unwrapped the parcel.

They sat in matching armchairs in the living room inside the Natsume mansion. A chandelier hung from the vaulted ceiling over a black-and-white checkered floor. Sunlight streamed in from the windows, illuminating the elegant furnishings and affording Masako the beautiful solemnity of a statue.

"I did," Himari answered hastily, seated across the table from her. "You're welcome to have some if you'd like. No worries if not." She fully expected her gift to be rejected and wasn't too broken up about it.

In the service of having a serious conversation, Himari was dressed in a beige crew-neck sweater over a white round-collar shirt dress, thick black leggings, and a pair of Mary Janes. Adorning her long hair was a pin decorated with a small gold ribbon, and as a token of goodwill, she brought a gift of freshly baked cookies. One might think it strange of her to bring baked goods to someone who previously tried to attack her, but it was a thank-you gift for the pudding, which the penguins devoured with relish.

"Does Kanba eat these cookies?" Masako asked in a tone of forced calm. She wore a dark green velvet dress with a large, luxurious black ribbon on the chest. Beneath it was a pair of sheer black plaid tights and brown ankle boots. She didn't consider Himari to be on her level whatsoever, but truth be told, when she first saw the girl's outfit on the security cameras, she ran back and reapplied her perfume.

"Uh, probably? I mean, I left some on the table, so..."

This was Himari's first time ever seeing a real fireplace, and it was blowing her mind. A real fireplace with real fire and real wood! The orange flames were so powerful, they warmed up the entire room. It was very impressive.

"Is there something wrong with the fireplace?"

"Oh, no, it's just...I've never seen one in real life before. I've only ever read about them and seen them in movies," she admitted, staring at her lap in mild embarrassment.

"How very odd you must be to bring me a gift," Masako commented without batting a lash. She grabbed one of the cookies and put it in her mouth. "Well, they're perfectly edible." Then she rose to her feet, strode to the nearby cupboard, and looked up at the tea set sitting on top. "No objections to Assam tea, I presume?"

You're an odd duck yourself, you know, Himari thought to herself. Not only had Masako actually eaten one of her cookies, but now she was making them both some tea. Hard to believe this was the same terrifying girl who fired a slingshot gun at her.

"I remembered the truth," Himari began vaguely.

"Yes, I'm aware. And there's still so much more you ought to know. That's why I called you."

Himari straightened her posture and waited for her to continue.

"Kanba and I are siblings by blood." Masako set two dainty little patterned teacups down on the table beside the gilded plate of cookies and poured hot Assam tea into each.

"You are?" Himari asked. Now that she thought about it, they both had sharp, analytical eyes and upturned noses. "Then why...?"

She was aware that Kanba wasn't born into the Takakura family, but she never thought too hard about where he came from. Why would he choose to live at the Takakura house when he had a real family right here in this mansion?

"To make me the sole heir to the Natsume legacy. He chose to stay there with our father for my sake and Mario's. Because he loved us."

And it was that love that she came to reclaim when she visited the Takakura house. Kanba's love once protected the Natsume family, but now it was being directed at Himari and Shoma instead.

Masako looked at Himari with her hard, almond-shaped eyes, but the other girl simply averted her gaze quietly. With a small sigh, Masako set the teapot on the table. "At least now you surely understand how entitled you've been acting."

Himari couldn't say a word. Her beloved older brother spent all this time looking after some other family's children while his *actual* sister suffered alone—indeed, one could tell they were related. But were Kanba's choices really *her* fault? Was she meant to apologize to Masako? She wasn't sure. She and Shoma simply accepted, respected, and loved Kanba as one of their own. Was that such a crime?

"Because of you, Kanba has been putting himself in danger." Masako curled her slender fingers around her teacup and lifted it to her lips.

"What sort of danger?"

"He's been cooperating with the remnants of KIGA, the organization behind the bombing sixteen years ago."

This confirmed what she went into the ramen shop to find out. The journalist was telling the truth: Kanba was indeed accepting money from that organization.

"For my medical expenses...?" Himari whispered sadly.

This infuriated Masako. How could this girl possibly sit still at a time like this? She planted herself right up against the back of the armchair, and her feet couldn't even reach the floor. Everything about her was so utterly childish—her round face, her tacky hairpin, her lanky limbs, her flat chest. Even her manner of speech was childish!

Over the years, Renjaku showed Masako countless surveillance images of Himari, and yet for some reason, now that the girl was sitting right in front of her, resentment flared up inside her all over again. "Isn't it obvious?!" she snapped without entirely meaning to. "He's doing it all for you!"

Kanba spent *years* waiting hand and foot on this little child, wasting *years* of his precious life using women as a crutch while he ate these plain, plebeian cookies and pretended to be happy, all the while making his *actual* sister live alone in this giant house.

"What should I do?"

It wasn't clear whether Himari was actually asking *her* or if she was asking herself. The longer they sat here, the more likely this girl was going to take over the conversation. But she wasn't malicious—just stupid.

"You and I are going to stop him together. Otherwise Kanba might just cross a line that can never be uncrossed."

Together was less than ideal, but she had no choice. Without Himari's cooperation, Kanba likely wouldn't listen to a word she said. But more than that, after meeting the girl in person, Masako learned one important thing about her: she clearly cared about Kanba in her own way.

School was no place to have a private conversation with Kanba, but we couldn't have it at home either, since Himari was there. So after she went to sleep, I led him outside to the empty lot beside the house. When I first told him I wanted to talk, he must have noticed my duffel coat and realized it was going to take a while, because he went and fetched his black military jacket.

"It's freezing. What do you want?" Kanba plopped down on an animal-shaped playground fixture and looked up at me as I stood there, staring at the ground.

I was seething, so I cut to the chase: "Why did you lie to us?"

"What are you talking about?" he asked without batting an eye.

"Himari's medical expenses. Where are you *really* getting the money?"

I was so sure that random journalist was lying—that our brother was more trustworthy than a total stranger—but then I saw the *photos*. And if the journalist was telling the truth, then it would seemingly explain why I sensed that something shady was going on. But more importantly...he knew that we weren't actually his real family.

"Does it matter? We needed the money. End of story."

We both exhaled the same foggy breath in the same shade of white, but it still felt like there was a massive gulf between us.

"Aniki, are you seriously taking money from those people?"

In the best-case scenario, he would deny it with a laugh, tell me I was clearly half-asleep, and send me back into the house to change into my pajamas. But I already knew I wasn't going to get the best-case scenario. There was no other way any of us could possibly get our hands on that kind of money.

"I met a journalist today. He knew everything about our family, including where you're getting your money. He asked me how I felt about it."

"So what?"

His voice was so calm and cold, it made me grimace in

frustration. But what exactly was so frustrating? The fact that he wasn't panicking? The fact that he kept something this important from the two people who were supposed to be his family? Or was it the fact that he tried to shoulder the burden by himself when he knew *full well* he shouldn't? Honestly, probably all of the above.

"What are you *thinking*? I know damn well you haven't forgotten the magnitude of our parents' horrific actions. And now you're taking money from their *cronies*? Screw you!"

I couldn't possibly risk letting Himari find out about this. How would she react? Neither of us was prepared to have that conversation.

"How else would you like me to pay for her treatment, Shoma? Because I don't see any other options!"

He glared at me, and I faltered. No, there were no other options—I understood that. Without that money, Himari would have died by now—I understood that, too. But these were two very separate problems.

"Just stay the hell away from them. And obviously, don't breathe a word of this to Himari. Problem solved."

"No, it isn't!"

Ignorance was not bliss, though I used to tell myself it was. When we broke into Oginome-san's home and rooted through her stuff, I averted my eyes, stuck my head in the sand, and tried to convince myself it was all for Himari's sake. Likewise, Kanba said the same thing. But I didn't actually believe that at all. Bad things were objectively bad; the ends did not justify the means.

"Then how are *you* gonna get the money, huh? How are *you* gonna save Himari?" he shot back flatly. "There's only one way we can save her. We have to change this corrupted world."

The familiar words sent a chill running down my spine. "What are you *talking* about, Aniki?"

"I'm gonna save Himari, no matter what. You just sit there and watch me."

"Like hell I'm just gonna sit there! You're going about it the wrong way!"

"Oh yeah? Am I?" he asked defiantly. I didn't know what to say to this. Clearly he thought I was powerless...

"Damn you!"

I lunged at him, swinging my fist. But I had no prior experience in fistfights, and he dodged my attack with ease. Before I slammed my face against the animal-shaped fixture, I hastily braced myself with my hands. Then, with a groan, I pushed myself back up and went for him again. He grabbed my fist in his palm and twisted my arm; the sudden pain made me grimace.

"You're wasting your time."

I knocked his hand away and swung at him again.

"You're wasting your time!"

This time Kanba punched me hard in the jaw, knocking me onto my back. The world started spinning, and lights popped behind my eyelids—so bright, you'd think it was daytime.

"Aniki," I groaned, forcing myself up into a sitting position even though I still couldn't see straight.

"Aniki?" he retorted sarcastically. "Please. Don't address me like I'm your brother. We're just two strangers who happened to be born on the same day," he snorted.

Did he really think of us as strangers? Even if we weren't actually blood-related, could he really turn around and call me and Himari "strangers" when we spent all these years living together like family?

"You and me and Himari—we've never been family, not once. And Shoma, you can't save her."

I thought of him as my brother, but after that, I was done calling him Aniki.

"Looks like this is as far as we go. Now our ties have finally been severed. This has all been dragging on for way too long, anyway."

"We...we're family, aren't we? Our ties can't be severed!"

He turned his back on me and looked up at the rainbow-colored wall of the house, its vibrancy dimmed in the twilight.

"So tell me about this journalist. What did he look like?"

As I sat there on the ground, he crouched down and grabbed me by the collar. The look in his eyes was cold and hard, nothing like the Kanba I was so used to. Wordlessly, I examined his features. Then, with a sharp glare, he relinquished his grip on me and strode off down the street.

"Where are you going?!"

But he didn't answer. Instead, he vanished into the darkness of night.

I forced myself up onto my feet. There were a few small black stains on the navy blue fabric of my coat; I wiped at them with my palm and realized it was blood. Then I noticed the taste of metal in my mouth.

"Sho-chan?" a feeble voice called out.

Startled, I looked up to find Himari crouched down on the porch, clutching her pink pirate teddy bear tightly in her arms, staring at me in shock. Then she stepped down off the porch and walked over to me, barefooted.

"You're bleeding. We need to patch you up," she continued in a watery voice.

How long had she been watching our exchange?

"Kanba left, and he's probably not coming back. Let's just stop here."

"*Stop*? Stop what?" Her eyes filled with tears.

"Let's stop pretending to be a family." Except to me, it was never pretend. "You can blame it all on me. The Takakura family ceased to exist a long time ago... I can't keep pretending it didn't."

"Are you serious about this?"

"Kanba's gone, and now we've got that journo sniffing around. Staying in this house will only prolong our suffering. C'mon, Himari, let's call it quits."

"I'm not suffering!" Shaking her head, she grabbed the sleeve of my coat. "And I'm sure Kan-chan will come back, so—!"

"Tomorrow I'll get in touch with Uncle Ikebe. You're going to go stay with him."

Himari was on the verge of tears, but she didn't let them fall. She just stared at me for a long moment. Then, quietly, she nodded. "Okay."

How sorely I wished I could take it all back, tell her it was a bad joke, and endure the silent treatment as punishment for the next three days. How I wished I could pretend that Kanba would come home tomorrow morning when he got hungry.

"Come on. We need to disinfect the wound," she said quietly. Pulling me by the sleeve, she led me back to the porch, where she had left the sliding door wide open.

She was surely freezing to death wearing only a nightgown, and her expression was grim; it reminded me of the day I first met her. Yes...I was the one who made Himari a co-conspirator in the Takakura family's crimes. And if we hadn't taken Kanba in, he wouldn't have had to pay the price in my stead. So really, this was for the best. No matter how badly it pained me, in the end, all that mattered was getting Himari to safety.

Inside, she pulled on a cardigan and some socks. Then she turned the light on in the living room and examined my face, her eyes wide.

"He really got you good, Sho-chan." I knew she was sad, but she forced a smile nonetheless. "That's what you get for starting fights," she continued, and I could hear the tears in her voice.

"That bad, huh? I hope it doesn't swell up too much or else I'll never hear the end of it at school tomorrow." My voice was so calm and quiet, it threatened to disappear into the tatami beneath me.

With her small, dainty hands, she poured disinfectant onto a cotton ball—"This is going to sting"—and pressed it against my lip. Sure enough, it stung like hell. It hurt so bad, I wanted to wail and scream. But I knew if I started crying, she would join in, so I suppressed it. Because that was what a good brother did.

Tabuki stood outside a ramen shop on the outskirts of town. Summoning his resolve, he opened the door. At last, he tracked down the last known hiding place of Takakura Kenzan and his wife Chiemi. It wasn't even that far from the house where their children lived.

"Here? Really?" he muttered to himself. The interior was pitch-black, with no signs of human life. The whole place was covered in dust and spiderwebs—hard to say whether it had electricity or even plumbing. Hesitantly, he moved deeper inside. The reek of mold was overwhelming.

Then he glanced behind the counter and sucked in a breath.

"It can't be..."

There lay two skeletal corpses, side by side, wearing sun-faded orange jackets with the KIGA emblem on the back. Reflexively, Tabuki grabbed the jacket and lifted it slightly. The name "K. Takakura" was neatly sewn into the chest pocket in navy blue thread.

"God..."

Takakura Kenzan was dead, and the skeleton beside him was probably Chiemi. The monsters Tabuki had chased after for so long had already met their end, right here. What was he supposed to do now?

At no point had Takakura Kanba actually met with his father Kenzan. It simply wasn't possible. Was this the place where he died, or had someone merely dumped his body here after retrieving it from elsewhere? Tabuki had no way of knowing. It could take any-where from a week to several months for a human body to fully decompose, depending on temperature and other factors. Judging from the earthy color of the bones, these corpses didn't look fresh.

"I always had a feeling Takakura Kenzan was dead."

Startled, Tabuki whirled around, bracing himself. Then he quietly let out the breath he was holding. "Yuri! What are you doing here?"

"Ironic, isn't it? Turns out we already got our revenge a long time ago. We just didn't know about it."

Yuri was standing there, dressed in a collarless camel coat. In the darkness of the filthy abandoned restaurant, her face and hair glowed like an angel's.

"You're such a handful. I've been looking all over for you."

He took a deep breath, then opened his mouth in preparation to say something, but the words wouldn't come. He assumed she would have forgotten about him by now in her one-woman quest to find Momoka's diary. Additionally, he found it odd that none of the news channels were reporting on the famous Tokikago Yuri's failed marriage, but hadn't thought too hard about it.

"Now then, let's go home where we belong. This marks the end of our first couple's spat." She held out her hand, her skin as beautiful and white as snow.

"Home..." Slowly, Tabuki reached out to take it.

But just then, a figure in a black coat ran in from outside and slammed into them. When they pulled away, blood splattered to the dusty floor.

Just like that, their family reunion was over, without even a scream.

Unsurprisingly, Uncle Ikebe agreed to take Himari in. I didn't tell him about Kanba or the journalist—instead, I said I felt Himari would be better off living with people who could look after her properly. Going forward, it was possible she could actually attend school in between hospital visits, at which point she would need a grown adult to sign the paperwork. Really, this was for the best.

Over the course of a few days, Himari packed her travel bags full with as much as she could carry. Then, on the day of her departure, she woke up bright and early to make an uncommon breakfast: eggs, toast, soup, and salad. The sky was clear, and the sunshine was warm.

Sleepily, I sat across the table from her, watching her long lashes sparkle in the morning light as I stuffed my mouth full of toast. She was dressed in a frilly blouse and a blue flared skirt; her long hair was thoroughly brushed and tied back with her favorite ribbon. Why was she wearing her Sunday best on a day like this? I didn't understand.

Our final few days together were unusually quiet. I looked in the mirror and was horrified to find a fat purple bruise running down my left cheek to my jaw. Hastily, I cleaned and iced it. Then Himari asked me for a handful of recipes she hadn't quite memorized yet, so I recounted them to her, and she wrote them down in her notebook. "Thanks," she said with a slight smile.

Since Uncle Ikebe probably wouldn't be able to see Penguin No. 3, she told me she was going to stop playing with it and acknowledging its presence. After all, if she tried to keep doing it in secret, they might think she smuggled in a pet. Neither of us said a word about Kanba.

"Well, I guess I should go now." Himari pulled on her boots, then opened the sliding door and peered outside. She was wearing a thick fur coat with white trim and a cape, carrying a large bag, with No. 3 at her feet.

"Okay."

She was smiling, but I couldn't.

"Here, Sho-chan. Thanks for everything." As she spoke, she opened her bag and pulled out a ratty old striped scarf, its colors dull and faded.

"You held onto it all this time?" It was the scarf I lent her, back before we were ever family, and I hadn't seen it since.

"This scarf tied us together, but now I'm giving it back to you. Now we're officially strangers." Smiling, she pushed the scarf into my hands.

"I'm sorry." My fingers tightened slightly, clutching the soft scarf, and I stared at the floor. Apologies wouldn't fix anything at this point. We were both in the process of losing our only family.

"It's fine. We're strangers now."

Confused, I looked up at her. Her eyes were swimming with tears, and yet she was still smiling somehow.

"The truth is, I always loved you, right from the start. But...I'm not a good girl."

I wanted to call her name, but before I could, she ran right up to me, got up on her tiptoes, and kissed my lips. When she pulled away, tears started rolling down her cheeks. Then she dashed out the door, slid it shut behind her, and was gone, without so much as a goodbye.

Alone, I stood there, staring down at No. 2 as it swooned on the welcome mat.

Back when the house was occupied by three teenagers and three penguins, it felt cramped. Then when Kanba left, it got bigger all of a sudden. Now that I was alone, the house was massive, silent, and empty. Everything they left behind had lost its color. The penguin hat was no longer sitting on the globe; apparently Himari took it with her. That family outing at the aquarium felt like centuries ago.

Kanba's belongings were all still here, as were more than half of Himari's, but everywhere I looked—the corner of the hallway, the red curtains, the entryway—the reality that they were never coming back stared me in the face.

Every time I did the laundry, there was barely anything to wash. As the old machine rumbled and rattled, I opened the lid and gazed down at its contents, swirling with detergent suds. When we were young, Himari and I always loved to watch the washing machine. Together, we'd climb onto a stepstool just to watch the clothes spin. "How is that any fun?" Kanba would always ask. Then our mother would tell us to stop doing it because it wasn't safe.

To this day, I still couldn't explain what made it fun, but here I was. Except now I didn't need a stepstool, and there was no one around to worry about me or watch it with me. But here I was, watching...all the while reliving the sensation I'd felt against my lips.

Later, I hung up the wet laundry while the sun was still high in the sky. For lunch, I ate leftovers from last night's dinner. I didn't feel like cleaning, and I probably didn't need to go grocery shopping, since I'd only be cooking for one tonight. My sluggish body wanted nothing more than to lie down and do nothing, but it was still too early to pull out my futon on a weekend. Instead, my legs carried me to Himari's bedroom.

She would never sleep in this room again, so I could get rid of the fancy sheets and cushions, take down the canopy—hell, I could take the whole bed apart if I felt like it. If I customized it to suit my own preferences, I would no longer have to deal with the hassle of moving a futon in and out of a closet every day. As my mind wandered, I sat down on her bed. Likewise, Penguin No. 2 hopped up next to me and sat down.

The bed was surrounded by large cardboard boxes full of summer clothes, books, sewing tools, plush toys, scrapbooks, colored pencils, and a cookie tin that contained her button collection. I needed to write her name and new address on a packing slip, take them to a package delivery company, and have them sent to my uncle's house.

"Oh..."

On top of the sheets lay a single photograph: one of me, Himari, and Kanba as kids. We were all grinning from ear to ear, standing in front of the wall we'd just finished painting. Kanba had an adhesive bandage on his right cheek, Himari was wearing her hair in pigtails, and I'd gotten a splotch of paint on the tip of my nose. It was the first photo we ever took as a family, just the three of us; as I recalled, we used a tripod and the self-timer function to make it happen.

"And now they're both gone."

I stared into space for a moment, and then the next thing I knew, I was sobbing so hard my face hurt. In the end, I passed out in the living room with only a single blanket.

By the time hunger finally woke me, the sun had nearly set. I crawled out of the blanket and went to fetch the clean laundry. As I brought it into the house, I rubbed my eyes and contemplated what to eat for dinner. Then I watched No. 2's round belly rise and fall as it slept nearby, and it occurred to me that I should probably check the weather forecast for tomorrow. Only then did I finally remember to turn on the television after days and days of forgetting it even existed.

"It's cold…"

I no longer had to go out of my way to cook anything special. It didn't really matter what I ate, as long as it was warm and filling. With that thought, I switched over to the cooking channel.

"Oden stew? Yeah, right."

Oden was not something you cooked for a single person. As I stared blankly at the screen, time flowed like sand. Together, the chef and the female show host worked quickly to prepare a pot full of enough stew for four or five people. Then it was time for the taste test, and they gushed about how good it was, and then the show was over.

Naturally, my stomach was rumbling by that point. I knew I needed to eat something, but I was too lazy to do anything. Times like these, I wished the penguin would make me something as a token of gratitude for its caretaker. Then a news program came on, and I finally pushed myself up onto my leaden feet.

"Hey, wake up."

I poked No. 2 with my toe, but it simply rolled over and went back to sleep. With a sigh, I headed to the kitchen. Then I overheard the phrase "near Ogikubo Station" and looked back at the TV, where the newscaster announced that a station wagon had flipped and crashed, killing the driver—a tabloid journalist.

They showed images of the scene taken by an eyewitness on their cell phone, and sure enough, it was the same station wagon the journalist I spoke to was driving, except now it was upside-down, exuding smoke, and fused with a telephone pole. The newscaster explained that the car hadn't actually collided with anything—it just spontaneously rolled into the pole. This impact crushed the driver, killing him instantly. This journalist was in the middle of an investigation at the time of his death, but the details were unknown. For the time being, the police cordoned off the street with yellow tape to investigate the initial cause of the crash. Then the newscaster addressed a reporter live on the scene.

"Kanba...?"

I didn't want to believe it, but...that journalist was in the middle of investigating our family, and the three of us were the only ones who knew about it... Gingerly, I reached up and touched the spot where Kanba punched me, still faintly swollen. Then I thought about the cold, hard look on his face when he demanded to know what the journalist looked like. If he went off to be with the terrorists, then this was no accidental death.

All this time, no matter what moral boundaries Kanba crossed, we always respected him as our brother. But that was because we believed wholeheartedly that he would never do anything worthy of more than a facepalm and a scolding, and we trusted him not to take it too far. There was no reason to doubt him, and so we forgave him for all of it. But if Kanba had gone beyond the point of no return, then our relationship was truly over for good. I would never be able to forgive him for that.

I realized a tear was rolling down my cheek, but I didn't wipe it away. Instead, I ran into the bathroom and puked in the toilet. I couldn't control it; it felt like something was squeezing my organs from my chest to my gut. My teeth chattered. And in that moment, it finally hit me: no matter how far apart we were, we were still a family. No matter which of them came home, no matter how long it took them, we would surely go right back to our lives together.

But that day would never come. Neither my words nor Himari's feelings would ever get through to Kanba. We were strangers now. All of us.

Looking back, it was probably KIGA that held the funeral for his father. Kanba was still just a boy at the time, and as he stood there in front of the coffin, he quietly wondered what would happen to him. His father had cut himself off from the Natsume family, and Kanba made the choice to go with him. Now he was all alone.

"This man was one of our dear compatriots," Takakura Kenzan declared, tears in his eyes. *Whoa.* The guy was even more emotional than Kanba himself.

Kenzan was one of the organization's executives; he brought his wife and two children to the service. The kids were close in age to Kanba himself, and in fact, he'd seen the older brother at the office on occasion.

Kenzan and his wife Chiemi both looked at Kanba with sympathy.

"You have nothing to worry about, Kanba. Starting today, we're your new family," Kenzan declared, so matter-of-factly that he couldn't argue.

His father always seemed to regret taking him away from the Natsume family. Whether he thought of him as a burden or simply wanted him to be with his siblings, it wasn't clear. But he would always say the same thing: "I failed at family." Kanba's mother was driven away by his grandfather's tyranny, and since his father lacked managerial skills, he couldn't stay long, either. Did he end up in KIGA afterwards, or did he leave the family *because* he joined KIGA? Kanba didn't really know.

Naturally, Kanba himself was part of the "family" his father had failed at. They were two failures, living a failed life together. Did his father ever really love him? Did he love his father? Was he even mourning at all? As he stared down blankly at the ground, Chiemi walked over, dressed head to toe in black, and crouched down to meet his eye level.

"I swear, Shoma talks about you all day every day. Don't worry, Kanba-kun—it doesn't take long to fit in with us. You'll be their big brother before you know it."

No grown-up had ever smiled at him like that. Judging from her friendly tone and the slight distance between them, he could tell she was trying to be respectful of his space. But even then, he doubted it would be that easy to join someone's family. Even his real family got angry and shouted at each other.

Chiemi led him by the hand out of the funeral home to the crematorium. Behind them walked Kenzan, Shoma, and the other girl. At the time, his only thought was: *I didn't realize Shoma had a little sister, too.*

As his father's body burned to ash, he sat at a table in the waiting room with the Takakura family and silently ate the packed lunch he was given. It wasn't especially tasty or gross—it was just normal food. It didn't taste like anything.

"Look at you, eating your veggies! I'm proud of you," Chiemi told him.

Kanba didn't know how to respond to this. Shoma finished everything except his snow peas, but his sister barely touched anything. Her complexion was wan.

"Himari, you don't have to push yourself," Chiemi told her gently.

"Okay," the girl, Himari, answered quietly. After a sip of tea, she continued, "Thank you for the food."

"Yeah, thanks for the food," Kanba hastily chimed in, almost like an afterthought. Then Himari glanced over at him, and for a moment, their eyes met. She had big, round eyes—*just like Shoma,* he thought to himself.

It wasn't until they asked him what he wanted to do with the bones that it finally sank in: his father was dead. His father's dead body was reduced to bones, and now tradition dictated that the next of kin use chopsticks to pick them up and put them in a funerary urn. But Kanba was still a child. He wasn't in charge of this funeral.

"Whatever you decide, make sure you won't regret it. Your father was a great man," Kenzan told him.

And so Kanba decided to look at his father's bones.

There were no identifying features left—just an arrangement of slightly yellowed human bones. As the undertaker stood at the ready nearby, he stared down at the pieces in contemplation. Even if his father thought of him as a burden—even if the man had died cursing his failed family—he decided he still loved his father all the same. No particular reason.

As he broke down crying, Shoma flinched in surprise. "You okay?"

Was he? Kanba didn't know the answer. Deep down, he was terrified of joining Shoma's family. Suddenly, he felt something cold against his cheek. Startled, he touched it and realized something was stuck to his face, right over his tear streak.

"See? We match," Himari explained, holding up her index finger to show him the bear-patterned adhesive bandage wrapped around it. "Now it won't hurt anymore, right?"

Tilting her head, she looked at him in concern. She was a pale girl, clad in black shoes, black tights, and a black dress.

"Did that fix it?"

"Yeah, I'm okay." He was so startled, he stopped crying. Instead, he offered Himari a small smile.

After that, Kanba became a Takakura kid—the older brother of Shoma and Himari. And at some point along the way, he vowed to himself that he would protect Himari at any cost. He would never let anyone destroy his family ever again. She was his beloved baby sister, and he was going to save her.

"I'm gonna save you, I promise." Kanba looked over his shoulder at Himari, knees tucked to her chin, sitting among the black teddy bears stacked up to the ceiling.

"Okay," Himari nodded, smiling. "I'm with you to the end, Kan-chan."

In return for all the times Kanba protected her, Himari decided it was her turn to watch over him. That was what brought her here. She didn't fully understand what he was talking about when he said he would "save" her, but she could plainly see that he was plotting something with KIGA, talking to them through these computer monitors all day every day. And whatever they were plotting, it wasn't good.

There was a small KIGA symbol affixed to the door, and the eyes of the teddy bears gleamed an ominous shade of scarlet. Plus, there were the men in black that kept coming in and out. They were nice enough, but for some reason, it felt like they were pulling Kanba further and further away. There was no going back now. She had to stop him and rescue him from this place—at *any* cost, even her own life.

That morning, Dr. Washizuka had a very strange dream. When he opened the door to his exam room, he instead found a different, unfamiliar room—the sort of room that didn't belong in a hospital at all. When he stepped back out into the dark hallway to double-check, sure enough, the placard outside said it was his exam room...and yet it *couldn't* be. He didn't recognize the erratic mess of colors on the walls, or the fuzzy clock projected over it, or the porcelain-enameled furniture, or the wooden bookshelves. There was no trace of the room he himself was using.

"Welcome to my exam room."

Just then, he noticed a young man dressed all in white sitting on a stool nearby, his legs crossed, his long hair tied back, smiling faintly. His eyes gleamed brightly as he gazed back at Washizuka... but at the same time, it felt like the young man was looking *beyond* him somehow. Beside him stood two young boys wearing dark clothing, their expressions perfectly blank.

"What are these children doing here?"

The boys looked back at him with bright red eyes.

"Good evening! Or good morning, as the case may be," the longhaired man greeted him leisurely. "Please, have a seat."

"Good evening," Washizuka replied as he sat down on the stool usually reserved for patients.

Why did everything appear so fuzzy in this dream? Was it because he didn't wear his glasses to bed? In that case, why did the floor beneath him feel so firm when he was walking down the hallway? Surely there was no way he would get lost on the way to his own exam room.

"Forgive the sudden question, but...how do you feel about ghosts, Doctor?" the man smirked.

"Do they exist?!" shouted one of the boys.

"Are they scary?!" shouted the other. They giggled.

"Well, I'm a doctor, you know. I'm not well-versed in matters beyond the realm of science," Washizuka replied, feeling around to try to figure out whether he was wearing pajamas or scrubs. If he could find his pocket, he could get to his glasses case.

"Ah, of course. You see, I know a boy who claims to have met one. He said they had a conversation," the man whispered in a low voice, like he was telling a spooky story.

"It was probably an audiovisual hallucination induced by strong feelings or desires." Once again, Washizuka scanned the dimly lit room. He could faintly smell an array of medicines, plus some sort of flowery perfume. "Incidentally, I thought this room was my exam room, but apparently not. My, this is a rather vivid dream."

"I apologize. While you were off in Germany, I did a bit of redecorating. What do you think? Lovely, isn't it?" the man asked. The boys promptly started clapping.

"Lovely!"

"Stunning!"

"Oh... Sorry, but I'm afraid I'm not wearing my glasses at the moment—I can't even tell if I'm wearing my lab coat. But eh, it's just a dream, so I suppose it doesn't matter."

"That's not good, Doctor. There's something I need you to see."

"Yes, well, I'm afraid it's all rather fuzzy without my glasses."

The next instant, Washizuka's vision suddenly sharpened. The sense of discomfort he'd felt upon entering the room was gone, and his old exam room was back the way it used to be. The only decoration on the crisp, clean walls was a calendar from a pharmaceutical company; in the penholder was his favorite ballpoint pen. The desk, the medical exam table—all of it was reverted to match the cold, sterile furnishings found in any other exam room in this hospital. The mysterious boys had vanished as well.

"Now look at this photograph. Really takes you back, doesn't it?"

The man held up a framed photo. Washizuka took it and scrutinized it with the help of his trusty glasses. "Is that...?"

It was a group photo taken at the South Pole. Among them was a man with a stoic expression, holding up a peace sign; Washizuka recalled seeing him on television often.

"Not him—the one on the side."

On the far edge of the group was a beautiful man with long hair, wearing a fur coat and holding up a peace sign, just like the others. The memories came flooding back, and Washizuka let out a long sigh. "Right... It was quite a long time ago now. He was a very talented assistant of mine, but then he became the leader of a criminal organization, committed a large-scale atrocity, and ultimately died in the process."

"I was so close back then. But Momoka-chan got in my way, that little cutie," the man laughed, snatching the photo frame out of Washizuka's hands.

"Wait, what? Are...are you Sanetoshi-kun?"

Sanetoshi was the name of Washizuka's former assistant, depicted right there in that very photograph. He was a tall man, perpetually smiling, with androgynous facial features and long hair loosely tied back.

"What are you doing here? Am I dreaming about you? But why?"

"Because I'm a ghost," Sanetoshi grinned in amusement.

"A ghost?"

Washizuka furrowed his brow. To be clear, the Watase Sanetoshi he knew passed away many years ago, which meant this had to be a ghost or a hallucination of some sort. But if this was a dream, then no real explanation was necessary.

"If ghosts are too unscientific for you, then let's say I'm a curse. And now I'm back for round two." Sanetoshi recrossed his legs. Then he pulled a bright red apple out of nowhere and began to play with it, tossing it up in the air and catching it.

"What are you talking about?"

Washizuka remembered the day of the atrocity very clearly. And every day that followed, he asked himself: why would Watase Sanetoshi do such a thing? He thought back to how he had personally interacted with Sanetoshi, sometimes regretting everything, other times justifying it.

"I vowed to change the world, and now that intent has been passed down from my comrades to their children. Stunning, isn't it?"

"You know, I've never once forgotten you, but it's odd that I would dream about you *now*, of all times. I'm enjoying this little reunion, but...I see you haven't changed a bit," Washizuka muttered sadly.

Even in a dream, Watase Sanetoshi was up to no good. Many years passed as Washizuka struggled, and failed, to understand what made him tick. Unfortunately, this wasn't likely to change anytime soon.

"Now then, it's time for me to return your exam room back to you. Likewise, I enjoyed seeing you again, Dr. Washizuka. Good day to you." Quietly, Sanetoshi rose from his stool and bowed respectfully. Then he pulled off his lab coat, whirled it around like a cape, and vanished.

This dream was far more creative than Washizuka's imagination was capable of, and he started to worry about himself. But then again, it was just a dream. Before long, he fell into a deep sleep...and by the time he awoke to the sound of his alarm clock, he forgot that he dreamt at all.

PENGUINDRUM

CHAPTER 04

HIBARI AND HIKARI walked around the side of the house they'd visited countless times as children. One wore a white beanie, while the other wore a black one; both were wearing matching tortoiseshell sunglasses. They exchanged a glance.

"Looks like she's not home. What should we do? Put it in the mail slot?" Hikari asked, like the ditz she always was.

"But then she won't know it's from us!" Hibari argued. "Ugh, man, we didn't bring anything to write a note... What do we do...?"

If only they could leave a short note, they could simply put the gift in the mail slot and call it a day. But their true goal was to meet with Himari in person. They wanted to thank her for the scarves they were currently wearing.

"Should we just wait around somewhere nearby? It's really cold, though... Should we go buy some hot corn potage while we wait?" Exhaling a cloud of white fog, Hikari glanced around, but couldn't spot any vending machines in the vicinity of the Takakura house. "Or maybe some hot cocoa?"

"We can't just *stand around* or we'll be late for our next gig! Good grief, Hikari-chan, get it together!" With a small sigh, Hibari pondered their dilemma. They could try to come back next time they had some free time, but there was no telling when that would be. Besides, they couldn't be seen loitering around someone's house in these less-than-subtle disguises or else...

"Hey, you!" a shrill voice shouted, and they both nearly jumped out of their skin.

They whirled around to find a girl in a school-issued balma- caan coat standing there with her hands on her hips, glaring at them. She wore her hair in a casual bob cut, her sharp eyes peeking out from beneath her thick bangs, sizing the other girls up like prey.

"What business do you have at this house?"

Ringo took one look at these girls, dressed conspicuously in sunglasses and scarves, and determined that they were quite pos- sibly in league with that tabloid journalist. Or maybe they were journalists for some *other* publication. If so, then they probably came to snoop around without permission.

"We...we're not criminals!" Hikari blurted out, waving her hands.

"She never said we were! Now she's going to think we *are*!" Hibari hissed.

"Yeah, I do!" Ringo adjusted her book bag on her shoulder and stood her ground.

"Well, um...we're really not trying to cause any trouble," Hibari mumbled, faltering in the face of Ringo's intimidating glare. Reluctantly, she pulled off her hat and sunglasses, then nudged Hikari to do the same.

"Double H?!" Ringo yelped. It was the same ultra-famous kitschy pop idol unit she saw on billboards every day of her life—what on earth were they doing here? Her jaw dropped as she stared at the celebrity duo, currently clinging to each other with guilty looks on their faces. "Oh my god, it's really you!"

"We came to see Himari-chan," Hibari explained.

"We're old friends from elementary school," Hikari chimed in with a pained smile. "So yeah..."

But the three of them couldn't stay together forever. Thirteen years after the subway incident, sickly Himari became even sicker, and all the kids at school started to see the Takakura family in a different light. They were all unified against Himari, and neither Hibari nor Hikari could stand up to them. At the time, they were just as scared as everyone else. Himari's parents had committed a terrifying atrocity the likes of which they couldn't even imagine... and since Himari was their daughter, she was terrifying too.

"See, Himari-chan knitted these for us," Hibari explained, patting her scarf.

"As a token of friendship. She said she wishes us nothing but the best," Hikari chimed in, blinking back tears.

The teachers told them that Himari wouldn't be coming back to school due to her illness. The following year, Hibari and Hikari applied to an idol audition, then debuted as a two-girl unit. Their lives became fun and exciting, but incredibly busy, and although they never forgot about Himari, they eventually stopped talking about her. But she was always meant to be the third member of their group, standing right there alongside them.

"So we really wanted to see her in person and thank her for the scarves. This is our only chance..." Hibari looked away.

From Himari's perspective, perhaps their desires were extremely selfish. But Himari was precious to Hibari and Hikari, and they desperately wanted to make up for the cowards they had been as children. It was their one regret.

"Right," Ringo nodded sadly. "I'm sorry, but Himari-chan's not home at the moment, and she won't be back for quite a while."

She couldn't explain to them what was happening to the Takakura family—it wasn't her place. But Himari had left this house. That was all she could tell them for sure.

"Gotcha." Hibari and Hikari slumped their shoulders in disappointment.

"Sorry," Ringo repeated, feeling strangely guilty even though it wasn't her fault.

Hibari and Hikari exchanged a playful glance, just like they always did on TV. Then Hibari held out the little paper bag she was carrying. "In that case, could you give this to her for us?"

"It's our new album—we thought she might like to listen to it. We'll come back to thank her for the scarves another time."

The logo of their record label was printed on the front of the bag. Ringo took it and peered inside, where she could see a single CD wrapped up in a cute red ribbon.

"Okay, no problem. I'll give it to her, I promise."

In her eyes, Hibari and Hikari were taller, healthier, and far stronger than Himari. Sure, Himari was doing better lately, but compared to girls her own age, she was markedly different. Every part of her was small, or pale, or muted, or fragile...and Ringo didn't even know where she was.

"We named the album after the words that always meant the most to her."

After a forlorn farewell, Double H put their sunglasses and beanies back on, bowed politely, then jogged off down the street. They must have stopped by between gigs. Ringo waved goodbye, and as they disappeared into the distance, she let out a sigh.

"Oh, hi, Oginome-san," said a very familiar voice.

"Shoma-kun!" She whirled around to find Shoma trudging in her direction on leaden legs, carrying a grocery bag, his expression dead-eyed and defeated.

And so I told Oginome-san that Kanba and Himari had left the house. I needed to tell her *something*, after all—maybe not the full story, but given how frequently she liked to come over, she was bound to notice sooner or later. She was a treasured friend, especially to Himari, and right now, she was the only person I could talk to about my family situation. It was killing me to keep it all bottled up inside.

There was no one around to hear me say "This is delicious," or "That's hilarious," or "I'm tired," or "It's cold." And I was terrified that I would never get to share those feelings with anyone ever again.

"I went down to the police station with Uncle Ikebe to file a missing persons report," I muttered as I put the small amount of groceries I'd bought into the fridge.

"Why didn't she just go to your uncle's house like she was supposed to?" Oginome-san asked, sitting slumped over the coffee table, her book bag beside her, along with the "gift" she claimed to have received from Double H.

They were old friends of Himari's from elementary school, and at one point, Himari herself wanted to audition with them. I had no qualms with them wanting to thank her for the scarves she knitted, but given their history, I wasn't enthusiastic about the prospect, either. Himari struggled with her illness for *years*—they could have come to see her literally any time they wanted, be it at the hospital or right here at home. Himari would have been overjoyed to see them too; she would have thanked them with a smile on her face and tears in her eyes. But now she was nowhere to be found.

"What happened to that penguin hat?"

"Oh, the hat? Yeah, Himari took it with her."

And yet she left behind the things that tied us together—the pink pirate teddy bear and the old scarf. I sat down on the opposite side of the table, teapot in one hand, two teacups in the other.

"I was stupid. I should have paid more attention to Himari's condition, both physical and mental," I muttered to myself half-deliriously.

Oginome-san looked up at me with concern. "Still no word from Kanba-kun? I figure Himari-chan's probably with him."

Maybe so. But either way, Kanba refused to take my calls.

On the day Himari left...the day Kanba quite possibly killed someone...I wasn't feeling well, so I wrapped myself up in my blanket, flopped down on the tatami, and fell asleep without eating anything. Around midnight, I awoke to the sound of the phone ringing. The intense hunger made me feel even sicker.

"Hello?"

"Shoma? Did I wake you?" asked Uncle Ikebe, sounding a little rattled.

"Yeah, sorry... What's up?" I replied hoarsely.

"Himari was supposed to arrive today, right?"

"Uh, yeah...? Why?"

I looked up at the clock on the wall and checked the time. According to my uncle, he tried to call me several times before dinner, but I was dead asleep after all the crying and vomiting. Hastily, the two of us tried to track Himari down. I attempted to get in touch with Kanba, but he wouldn't pick up. *Figures.* Next, I called the hospital. A few seconds later, Dr. Sanetoshi himself picked up—no phone receptionist involved.

"Hello?" His voice was low, leisurely, and playful, just like always.

"Hi, uh, Dr. Sanetoshi? Sorry to call so late, but...um...Himari's gone missing, and I was wondering if she was with you."

"No, unfortunately, I haven't seen her," he replied apologetically. "I'm not sure where she could have gone."

"Yeah, me either. Sorry for bothering you, but I couldn't think of anywhere else."

"Oh, that's quite all right. Your sister doesn't have long left," he continued in a gentle, sympathetic tone that left me speechless. "So if you need to talk, I'm available anytime. Seems reasonable, doesn't it?"

"Hold on a minute! Wasn't your medicine supposed to cure her?!" I shouted.

"The thing about medicine is, the longer your body is exposed to it, the more resistant you become to its effects. Much like falling in love. Hadn't you heard?" I could practically picture Dr. Sanetoshi's smile, framed by his long rainbow-hued hair.

"The hell do *you* know about love?" I muttered before I could stop myself.

"Ah, you Takakura kids are all so very alike."

"So Himari...?" I fell to my knees, still holding the receiver.

"Yes, I'm afraid she's going to die soon," Dr. Sanetoshi replied offhandedly. And with that, he hung up on me.

My mind swam with dizziness and hunger and the memory of Himari's teary smile.

"Shoma-kun, you're looking kinda pale. Have you been eating enough?" Oginome-san asked suddenly.

"Oh, uh, yeah," I replied absently. "But I'm on my own right now, so I haven't made anything fancy."

Cooking for one was highly inefficient and not nearly as cost-effective. Plus, I generally wasn't motivated to make anything nice for myself.

"Okay then...what if I made you some curry or something?"

Oginome-san suggested tentatively as she sat up to take a sip of the tea I made. "Then again, curry's kind of the only thing I know how to make anyway."

"Good idea... I'll help. Otherwise I'm just going to forget how to cook anything."

I forced a smile. Times like these, the best option was to go all-out with tons of spices, grate up a ton of apples and ginger, and make a truly decadent dish. In winter it would keep for a quite a while, too, so we could safely make a big batch.

Oginome-san beamed. "Awesome! In that case, let's swing by the store later."

Right, of course. In times of emergency, I needed to make doubly sure *I* wouldn't get sick, too. I needed to keep living my life as Takakura Shoma—clean the house, do laundry, eat three square meals a day, do a little studying, and get a full night's sleep.

At this rate, with Oginome-san commenting on my complexion, I'd never find Himari...and if Dr. Sanetoshi was telling the truth, then I *really* needed to be by her side, spending the last few moments of her life as her former family.

Kanba continued to bring Sanetoshi money, no different from before. Regardless of whether he and Himari were living together, she would still need to go to the doctor either way. Sanetoshi took the envelope and checked the contents, but instead of pocketing the money, he tossed it down onto the desk. "Stunning, yes, but I'm afraid that medicine won't work anymore."

"The hell do you mean?"

Kanba jumped up from the stool and stormed over to him.

"Exactly what I said. The medicine won't work," he replied matter-of-factly, tilting his head. Faint blue and green lights rose up from his hair like steam, swirling together in a spiral.

"Then what'll happen to Himari?"

"She'll die," he answered, all too casually, and the lights popped.

"Gimme a freakin' break!"

After all that, it still wasn't enough? No matter how much money and how much of his life he offered in trade, he still couldn't save his beloved sister? Meanwhile, Sanetoshi smirked, enjoying Kanba's despair.

"I'll kill you," he choked out. Then he climbed on top of Sanetoshi and grabbed both of his slender, pale wrists, pinning him to the chair he was sitting in. But his captive didn't try to escape.

As Kanba tightened his trembling fingers, Sanetoshi's faint smile never faltered, nor did he groan in pain. Instead, he simply whispered, "You're wasting your time."

"I'll *kill you*!"

"What if there's still a way you could save your sister?"

As he gazed up at Kanba, he snapped his fingers, and two shadowy figures appeared behind him. Sensing their presence, Kanba slowly looked up—then relinquished his grip and staggered backwards a few steps. The look on his face was precisely what Sanetoshi anticipated.

There stood Kanba's dead parents, staring vacantly back at him.

"All you have to do is heed our curse," Sanetoshi declared,

quietly wishing he had a camera to capture the delightful expression on the boy's face.

As for Kanba, his only option was to comply.

At the KIGA hideout, Kanba sat in front of several large computer monitors, holding a discussion with a group of men in black. The room was practically overflowing with black teddy bears, and their numbers were steadily increasing.

"The time to act is finally upon us. Load each train with fifty teddies." Kanba looked around at each of the men in turn. "Do we have enough for every train line?"

"Production is underway and proceeding smoothly," one of the men replied.

"We need three hundred more. Make it happen."

"Understood. Survival Tactic!" he shouted, flashing a peace sign.

"Survival Tactic," Kanba parroted back quietly, averting his sharp gaze.

"Bad news!" another man shouted on a different monitor, holding a cell phone in one hand. "Apparently the pigs found the room under the *La Terre* sculpture in Ikebukuro. A portion of the planning data is still there!"

At this, the men appeared mildly unnerved. "We gotta delete it!"

"I'll handle that," Kanba told them without batting an eye, projecting the resolute confidence of a leader. The other men applauded him, but he didn't notice; he was already thinking about the next order of business.

Regardless of who led the organization, regardless of "talent," his task remained the same: change the world and save Himari. KIGA was merely a means to that end.

"For now, just make sure to produce enough teddies," Kanba muttered, then ended the transmission. The monitors all faded to black, and with the curtains in the room drawn, everything went pitch-dark. Pensively, Kanba walked among the stacks of teddies to a large armchair and sat down, his posture perfectly straight.

"Kan-chan," called a feeble voice as Himari slid her slender arms around his neck from behind.

"What is it?" he asked without looking over his shoulder.

"Oh, nothing. Just felt like it." She pressed her cheek to his and whispered, "We'll be together forever, okay?"

Over the past few days they'd spent together, no matter how many times she asked him to quit, he refused to listen. He was clearly concerned for her, asking about her condition and making sure she wasn't too cold, but when it came to what she wanted most, it was like he couldn't see it at all.

"I love you, Kan-chan."

Though they weren't blood-related, Kanba had always looked out for her and Shoma, and he was an important part of their lives.

"I realized I don't have to be afraid anymore. You were the one who showed me that, Kan-chan. And now I'm willing to do whatever it takes for the people I love."

But Kanba didn't flinch, nor did he afford her so much as a passing glance. The eyes that used to look after her now seemed vacant; it wasn't clear whether he was actually looking at *anything* anymore.

"I'm sorry... I can only imagine how much you've suffered all this time."

This outcome was the direct result of Kanba having to carry the Takakura family on his shoulders all the time. Truth be told, she and Shoma had picked up on this, but instead of acting on it, they took advantage of Kanba's kindness, single-handedly driving him to the brink of self-destruction.

"I made this choice," he replied in a low, quiet, almost emotionless voice.

"No. You made so many sacrifices...gave me a piece of your life... but I pretended not to see it." Her arms tightened around his neck.

"Tell me, Himari. Do you remember the day we became a family?" He quietly reached up and touched her feeble arm.

"Yeah, of course."

"You gave something to me that day."

"I did?" She tilted her head slightly, then buried her face against his back. His black clothes smelled of dust, but he was warm, and his scent was familiar.

"Don't worry about it. I'll save you, I promise."

"Stop. Don't put yourself in danger!"

No matter how tightly she clung to him, her strength would never exceed his. Still, she couldn't afford to let go, lest he cross a line that could never be uncrossed. And at that point, he would officially be a stranger to her.

"It doesn't matter if I die. Just stay here with me."

Kanba sucked in a breath and held it quietly. Was he listening to her? Or was he thinking about something else entirely?

"You, me, and Sho-chan."

She wanted to go back to the days when they were just three kids living in the Takakura house, waiting patiently for their parents to one day come home.

"I gotta go." Kanba rose from the chair, but Himari refused to let go.

"No!" she shouted, louder than usual. "Go *where*?!"

Startled, Kanba looked over his shoulder and met her gaze. "Let go of me."

She glared back at him. "I refuse!"

Then his expression faded, and his eyes grew vacant once more. "*Let go of me*," he repeated, grabbing her arms and easily extricating himself from her grip.

Hastily, Himari latched on once more. "No!"

For the first time, Himari discovered her stubborn side. All her life, she had never really put up a fight, choosing instead to let things go without making waves. But now, for the first time, she was being selfish. *Extremely* selfish.

With a conflicted sigh, Kanba slowly and calmly pulled her arms away. But she only clung tighter, hanging from his neck with her full weight. In the end, he was forced to drag her with him to the front door. Powerless to hold him back, she staggered along behind him on her tiptoes, quickly growing out of breath. Then, after he opened the door, he extricated himself one last time, grabbing her by the arms this time.

"You are my everything. If you die, then the whole world is dead to me, too."

"Kan-chan!"

Himari inhaled sharply, her face contorted in fear. He pulled away from her, then walked out of the house without looking back. Left alone, she slumped to the floor, biting her lip as she struggled to catch her breath.

At the rate he was headed, Kanba would soon be too far gone to save. He was slowly retreating further and further into some scary place beyond the reach of his siblings. But there was still a way. Himari could still make a sacrifice for him, just as he had once done for her.

For the first time in her life, Himari entered the Sunshiny International Aquarium all by herself. She bought a ticket for one, then walked to the penguin enclosure.

If she could have rewritten her fate, perhaps she could have stopped Kanba from throwing his entire life away in the service of his family. Even if that was the destiny he chose for himself, maybe she could have chosen her *own* destiny. In her view, she was a weakling who relied on the kindness of others just to stay alive, so she didn't have the right to complain about what fate chose for her. But now she didn't really have a choice.

Like Masako said, Himari was acting incredibly entitled. Family or not, she couldn't rob Kanba of his life. Right now, Masako was taking action to save him; as for Himari, it was time she repaid them both.

"Look! Penguins!" a little girl shouted, dashing past.

"Settle down! No running!" her mother shouted, chasing after her.

Shoma and Kanba were acting strangely ever since their most recent trip to the aquarium. Kanba in particular seemed noticeably different. Since Himari was constantly in and out of the hospital, she just assumed they were walking on eggshells around her, but there were other changes, too. Like the delivery of the penguins, one of which now stood at her feet. Or the days when the boys would skip school or come home really late with no explanation. Perhaps if she'd kept her eyes peeled, she would have noticed even more oddities. Maybe then she could have prevented all this.

Now that she knew the truth, she was terrified of destroying those happy days. She never once imagined that hiding her true feelings would make everything *worse*.

"But that's my punishment," she muttered to herself as she approached the penguin enclosure. Her bare hands, unprotected by her white coat, were already flushed pink from the cold. The penguins didn't seem to mind the chill, however; they raced around in the water and gathered in tight groups on land, flapping their flippers.

She was being honest when she told Kanba she wasn't scared anymore. No matter what truth was waiting for her, even if she lost her life, there was nothing to fear. Her heart was chock-full of the precious memories Kanba and Shoma gave her. Thanks to them, every day felt like Christmas Eve in that she was always eager for the day that came next.

But from now on, she was going it alone. She needed to accomplish this goal with her own two hands. She was certain there had to be a God out there listening—and if not, she would just have to make one herself. She closed her eyes and clasped her hands together.

"Dear Lord, please return everything I stole from Kan-chan while pretending not to notice. Please help him. I'll give everything back—even my life."

As she spoke, a warm light shone out from between her fingers. This attracted the penguins' attention like a magnet, and they all wandered over to the edge of the enclosure, gazing at her.

"Take me back to that special day."

The warm light glinted off of her white coat, lighting up the vicinity so bright, she could no longer make out the penguins or the rest of the aquarium. Tears fell from her eyes, landing on Penguin No. 3, who collapsed on the spot. And when the light became so bright that she could no longer see herself, she quietly passed out.

God, if you're out there, please help him. I promise I'll never come back here again.

"Himari! Wake up, Himari!"

It was Christmas morning. Young Shoma shook Himari by the shoulders as she lay curled up under the toasty warm blanket. He was still in his pajamas, holding a neatly wrapped present that was left beside his pillow.

"Santa came to our house?" Rubbing her eyes, Himari rolled over and looked up.

"There's one for each of us," said Kanba as he carried hers over to her. "See? It says 'For Himari-chan' right there."

Back then, Himari didn't have her own bed yet. What would later become her private bedroom was currently the kids' room, where all three of them slept in futons. There was a small Christmas tree in the corner of the living room that she dearly enjoyed decorating with her brothers, using sparkly silver pipe cleaners, ribbons Chiemi saved from past gifts, little origami crafts in a rainbow of colors, and even a slightly warped *papier mâché* snowman.

"I can't believe it!" Himari sat upright, paying no mind to the chill as her little limbs left the safety of the blanket. Then she buried her face in her hands and giggled.

She never gave much thought to the concept of Santa Claus, but she loved the Christmas storybooks Chiemi would read to her, and when Kenzan told her that Santa would bring gifts to all the good boys and girls, she spent the entire month of December fiercely determined to be the best little girl she could be.

"I'm happy for you, Himari. See? I told you he could still get in without a chimney." A very bedheaded Kanba thrust out his chest proudly. He held Himari's gift in one hand and his own, much smaller gift in the other.

"So what did you ask for, Himari?" Shoma asked, blushing.

"Well..." Back then, what she *wanted* was a big, poofy princess dress with a glittery pale blue-layered skirt. But what she *asked for* was something entirely different.

"Himari?" Shoma tilted his head.

At the top of the little Christmas tree was a big yellow origami star. She already had a set of colored pencils that she took good care of, and as long as she had her pink teddy bear, she didn't need any other plush toys.

"Himari, what's wrong?"

Kanba offered her the gift box, wrapped in star-patterned paper with red and green ribbons. The three gifts were all different sizes, each with a card attached that had the recipient's name clearly written on it, and the room was filled with the chilly excitement of Christmas.

"I don't remember asking for something this big." Himari grabbed the box with both hands, raised it to her ear, and shook it. "Is my gift really in there?"

"Of course it is! You earned it for being good!" Shoma shouted excitedly.

"Yeah, Dad said so," Kanba chimed in.

"But..." She found it hard to believe. Had she really earned whatever magical gift was contained inside this giant box? Even then, there was no guarantee it was something she actually wanted.

"Oh, you're all awake," Chiemi commented as she slid the door open. Himari took one look at her mother's beautiful smile and started to cry.

"Mom, we got presents!" Shoma exclaimed happily.

"Himari's so shocked, she can't even remember what she asked for," Kanba laughed, shaking his head, as he crouched beside her.

"You can't remember? Oh dear. Well, you've been a very good

girl, so I'm sure it's something nice." Chiemi bent down and stroked Himari's hair.

"Really? Have I really been good?" she asked, anxious from the bottom of her heart.

"What's the matter, Himari? What are you so worried about?"

Chiemi smiled softly and stroked Himari's tear-soaked cheek with her soft, cool fingers. Meanwhile, the tears kept falling.

"Aww, sweetheart, why are you crying? I know for a fact you've been a good girl, and Santa knows it, too. Come here."

Himari sprang out of the futon and onto Chiemi's lap, clinging to her and breathing in the smell of her sweater until the fear (and tears) went away.

"Don't cry, Himari."

"You don't have to feel bad! Let's open the gifts!"

Her brothers came over to reassure her, and by that point her feelings swelled up so much that they started leaking out of the room.

"What's wrong?" Kenzan asked quietly, peering in through the open door. "Is Himari crying?"

"I'm afraid so. It sounds like she's scared that she didn't earn her Christmas present. Is that right, Himari?"

There in her mother's arms, she shook her head slightly. Truth be told, she *knew* she hadn't been a good girl. She knew about Shoma's fears and Kanba's suffering, but she didn't do a thing. She was powerless.

"I didn't, Mom. I'm not a good girl... Kan-chan left us... I was a bad girl, and now the whole family's split apart!"

In a blink, Himari was suddenly her teenage self again, sitting on the warm blanket, surrounded by her family from days gone by.

"There's nothing to cry about. Come on, let's all open our gifts together. There might be something fun in there!" Chiemi insisted matter-of-factly, smiling softly as she took Himari by the hand and reached for her gift.

"So what did you ask for?" Shoma repeated.

"Let's open 'em right now!" Kanba's small, warm hand gently cupped her face.

Himari slowly untied the ribbons and neatly peeled off the wrapping paper. Inside was a white box with a lid. Before she opened it, she glanced around at the others. They were all smiling at her.

"I'll try to be a good girl from now on," she mumbled as she lifted the lid. "So please..."

Her family cheered. Inside the box was a multitude of stars, shining so bright she could scarcely keep her eyes open, blowing her hair back, making it sparkle. Chiemi's distant voice lingered warmly in her ears: *See? You were such a good girl.* Enshrined in light, Himari's tears dried up.

I'll never call myself powerless ever again, she thought to herself. *I refuse to give up, even if it kills me.*

Yuri sat in a chair beside Tabuki's hospital bed, thinking about how he must have felt when he shielded her from the attack.

As far as she knew, the two of them were never in love, but...

that night at the ramen shop, when a black-clad Yuuki Tsubasa tried to stab her, Tabuki stepped in to take the blow. The knife sank deep into his gut, and when she pulled it out again, his blood chased after the blade, falling to the floor in an arc.

"How could you?!" Yuri screamed, glaring at Yuuki.

"It...it's not my fault! I loved you, but you betrayed me! In love and sin, you're always *baroque*!" Yuuki screamed, her complexion ashen.

"Then pick up that knife and stab me, too!" Yuri deeply regretted the way she had treated Yuuki's heart like a plaything, especially now that she saw the devastating repercussions of her faux-romance. "Either way, your life as an actress is over!"

Trembling, Yuuki fled the building, leaving the bloody knife behind.

"Tabuki-kun!"

Instead of chasing after Yuuki, Yuri bent down beside Tabuki and touched his wound. As he groaned in pain, she silently vowed to save him at all costs. She *needed* him.

"Yuri, I finally realized something," he said after a moment, forcing a smile, his forehead slick with sweat.

"Don't talk! You can tell me all about it later, so for right now, just hold on!"

If he had died at that moment, she probably would have followed suit shortly afterward. Never mind beauty or ugliness—she would have thrown it all away in a heartbeat. The memories of her time with him and Momoka were the only thing keeping Tokikago Yuri sane.

"You look so relaxed," she laughed to herself as she watched him sleep. Just then, he stirred awake. Their eyes met, and they smiled at each other.

"Did you say something?" he asked calmly.

"No, not at all. I was just thinking I wouldn't mind taking a bath with you."

She was wearing an oversized beige cashmere dress with black ankle-length leggings and black high-heeled ankle boots, and her hair was tied back in a tight ponytail—a modest look with no statement jewelry. She was wearing only a small amount of makeup with a gray-beige manicure. No wedding ring.

"What's that supposed to mean?" Tabuki snickered.

"I don't know. It was just a thought," Yuri replied, giggling along with him. "But you shouldn't laugh too much or your stitches will split open."

"Then don't make me laugh!" As he spoke, he reached over to the bedside table, grabbed his glasses, and carefully slid them up the bridge of his nose. "Yuri, I finally realized why we were the only ones who survived."

"And why is that?" Yuri asked as she peeled an apple with a paring knife.

"You and I were lost children right from the start—but in this world, most children are. That's why I needed someone to tell me they loved me, even just once."

Momoka must have instinctively sensed this using her special power. That was how she had the compassion to help so many people. And it was that mindset that he and Yuri needed to inherit.

When she received an invitation from Yuri to meet up in the hospital cafeteria, admittedly, Ringo hesitated for a moment. But she had a lot of questions about Tabuki Keiju and the diary, so ultimately she agreed to it. After school she usually got in touch with Shoma, but this time she decided to wait until after her little rendezvous.

"I apologize for making you come all the way out here on such short notice," Yuri said with a good-natured smile. Her neat ponytail and modest makeup afforded her a delicate appearance, reminiscent of the time they first met at Tabuki's apartment, especially the eyes and lips.

"No, that's okay. But, um..."

Ringo hadn't forgotten about Tabuki Keiju or the situation with Yuri. According to all the entertainment news programs, the wedding reception was postponed due to the groom's poor health, but rumor had it that Tokikago Yuri had already ended the marriage. Honestly speaking, Ringo foresaw that she would encounter her again sooner or later. Assuming she was still after Momoka's diary *and* the diary was still needed to save Himari, there would always be conflict between them...which was why she wasn't expecting it to be this peaceful.

"Believe it or not, Tabuki's upstairs in a hospital room as we speak," Yuri explained with a slight frown. Ringo's eyes widened.

"Wait, so when they said the reception was postponed due to poor health...?"

"Oh, that was a lie I told the media to buy myself enough time to track him down. I never meant for it to actually come true." Her long lashes fluttered as she looked away.

"What happened?"

"Just a couples' spat. Trust me, you don't want the details."

Something about her tone of voice set Ringo at ease. Apparently something happened between Yuri and Tabuki after the incident at the construction site...but that was *their* business, not hers. Besides, it seemed like they resolved it on their own.

"I know the two of us have put you kids through a lot, but I can promise you this: you won't have to worry about us anymore." As she spoke, she gently set half of Momoka's diary on the table. "So you can have this back. It took me a long time, but now I realize that Momoka wanted you to have it."

It felt like an eternity since Ringo last laid eyes on the diary. Gingerly, she reached out and took it. After all this time, had fate brought it back to her?

"Find the other half and complete the diary. Then you'll find the fate transfer spell written inside," Yuri explained intently.

"The fate transfer spell...?" Ringo looked down at the half-diary, trying to remember if she'd ever come across anything resembling a spell during her past read-throughs.

"Yes. If you use it, you can save someone you care about."

"I don't know... I've never thought about changing someone's fate."

"I'm not surprised. But Momoka entrusted this diary to you and you alone. She must have known you would need it someday."

Yuri's words resonated deeply in Ringo's heart. Her older sister, who was special and unique, had chosen *her* to inherit her diary. Surely there was some meaning in that.

Outside the hospital, the sky above her was chilly, but clear. With a smile, Ringo hugged the diary half to her chest and set off walking. Perhaps there was still something she could do to help.

Up on the rooftop of the office building, Kanba stood at the safety fence and glared down at Ikebukuro Station Square, one hand clutching at the chain links. His focus: the area surrounding the *La Terre* sculpture.

"The police have already caught on to your organization's little plot. They have eyes on you right this very moment." Masako stood behind him, dressed in a trench coat. "Now's your last chance to back out."

"I have to make this plan succeed. I have to save Himari's life," Kanba muttered to himself, as if he hadn't even noticed her standing there.

"And how do you intend to do that?"

Masako was reminded of something Sanetoshi once said to her: *Your parents failed to make their dream come true. So instead, I'm going to pass that duty down to their children.* And if her interpretation was correct, then that "dream" was another night-mare waiting to happen.

But Kanba didn't answer her question. Instead, he put his cell phone to his ear. "Look sharp. We've got an unmarked police car staking us out at the roundabout." His lips curled in a smirk as he listened to the reply. "All right, just leave it to me." With that, he hung up. Then, without so much as a glance in Masako's direction, he left the rooftop and headed back down the stairs.

She promptly followed suit, one hand holding her curls in place as the wind ruffled them. Ahead of her, Kanba's black jacket looked like a red-hot flame...but this time, she couldn't feel the heat of his burning passion. Not to suggest he was perfectly in control or anything of the sort—rather, that his fire was out of reach.

Arriving at the roundabout, Kanba slowly walked to the center, his eyes glued to his cell phone screen. Masako frowned, noting his unnatural behavior, and slowly trailed behind him.

"Kanba, what are you looking at?"

She peered at his phone screen and saw a basic CG image of the surrounding area. She looked up and glanced around. Sure enough, the buildings, cars, and pedestrians were all faithfully replicated in the image. Then Kanba tapped one of the parked cars, and its silhouette began to flash.

"What did you just do?"

Before he could respond, the resulting explosion made her duck down. When she looked up again, the parked car was lying on its side, exuding dark smoke.

"What have you *done*?!" she hissed. Panicked, she tried to snatch his phone out of his hands. "Stop it right now! That man is *using* you, Kanba! He won't actually help us!"

Kanba deftly evaded her hands. As he walked toward the *La Terre* sculpture, he tapped around casually, detonating every car in his way.

"Open your eyes, Kanba! This isn't right!"

All around them, the situation was slowly escalating. Using the smoke as cover, Kanba felt around for the little KIGA symbol carved into the base of the bronze statue. The door opened, and he slipped inside.

"Wait!" As sirens blared somewhere behind her, Masako ducked down and barreled through the door after Kanba.

The space inside the statue was too small to be called a room; all it contained was a single computer. In the darkness, Kanba pulled a jackknife from his pocket and jammed it into the system unit as hard as he could. Sparks flew, and the space filled with smoke. But Masako knew the computer wasn't his only objective. Maybe his job was done for today, but come tomorrow, he'd get dragged into an even bigger scheme…and she couldn't afford to let him add anything else to his list of crimes.

Desperate to calm her racing mind, she exhaled quietly. Her fingers brushed the slingshot gun concealed inside her pocket. If it came down to it, she was prepared to abduct Kanba by force. But right before she pulled it out—

"We have you surrounded! Cease all resistance and come out with your hands behind your head! I repeat: we have you surrounded!" a man's voice shouted over a megaphone—most likely a police officer.

"Kanba, we have to surrender. I'll come with you."

"*You* are going to drop your gun and go home. Just tell 'em I took you hostage or something."

As he spoke, he felt around on the floor with his foot, then pressed down hard. A small panel opened, revealing a secret spiral staircase leading down into the darkness. He started down the stairs without the slightest hesitation.

"Do *not* follow me."

But for Masako, no such option existed. She chased after him. "Where are we?"

"The Tokyo underground is a labyrinth of branching passageways. No map of them exists, and most of them haven't been disturbed for decades. This is one of them. Trust me, no one will find us in here."

"You really think you can outrun the police forever?" Her heels clacked on the stairs as they descended deeper and deeper.

"If that's what it takes to save Himari's life," he replied without missing a beat.

She stopped short. "Why are you doing this? She's just a stranger!"

And if you insist on helping her, then why won't you admit you love her?

"She's my sister."

No matter how emotional she became, Masako rarely ever lost control. Generally, she suspected that most of her anger died along with their grandfather. But emotions always found a way to reignite. She seized Kanba by the arm, digging her nails into his jacket, and yanked him back as hard as she could. As he whirled around to face her, she registered the look in his eyes, clearer and sharper than ever before.

"Look at me! *I'm* your sister!" she pleaded, gazing at him with narrow eyes that matched his, though hers were damp. "Snap out of it! That man has put a curse on us!"

But Kanba simply stood there in the darkness, silently enduring the pain of her fingers digging into him.

"I know you're aware of the vile, unspeakable things our father has done. And you saw where that got him."

All this time, Masako waited and waited for her father and brother to come home, all the while protecting Mario and protecting the Natsume family legacy. But her father never returned, and at this rate, Kanba wouldn't, either.

"Our dad is dead," he revealed to her without even batting an eye.

"That's not true."

Her grip on him weakened; he yanked himself free and continued down the stairs.

"That's *not true*!" She pulled out her gun and aimed it at his back.

"Yes, it is. He's been dead for more than eight years. You know this."

He heard the click of her gun, but didn't stop.

"All this time, I've been fighting to keep hold of everything I've got left. I refuse to accept that our father is dead, and I refuse to let them steal *you* away from me, too. If you don't stop, they'll use you and throw you away, just like they did to him! They'll crush you!"

"Don't care."

As she stood there, frozen, he walked off down the spiral staircase. She aimed a shot at the back of his head, but despite her best efforts, her laser sight was unsteady.

"I don't want to lose you a second time!"

Hands shaking, she fired the gun. The bullet missed by a wide margin, hitting the stairs ahead of him and breaking apart. Startled, he came to a stop and looked up.

"Say it. Say I'm your one and only sister. Say it just once, for old times' sake, and I'll commit to this curse with you for all eternity."

"Masako..."

For the briefest of moments, it felt like her fingertips grazed the fire burning inside him. Just then, a searchlight flared up, blinding them. Masako turned away reflexively. Kanba hastily leaned over the railing, peering down at the light shining up from below.

"There is no escape! Now give up and surrender! We have you surrounded! Cease all resistance immediately!" the policeman from earlier shouted over his megaphone.

Kanba crouched down, pulled out his cell phone, and started tapping around. "Get down," he told Masako, and a moment later, the sound of a rolling metal ball echoed through the vast underground space. She promptly crouched down next to him, listening to the sound.

"We have you both surrounded!" the policeman repeated, right before a deafening explosion filled the area, accompanied by thick smoke. As Masako clutched at her head in horror, a piece of ash landed on her hand, leaving a tiny burn mark.

As they arrived at the bottom floor, Masako gasped at the gruesome sight that awaited them. Kanba was controlling something that possessed far more offensive power than any measly slingshot gun—and with just his cell phone.

"Now maybe we'll have some peace and quiet," he remarked quietly as he scanned the bodies of the policemen twitching amid the smoke.

Masako's gun fell to the ground.

Perhaps Kanba was too far gone. Even then, she didn't care. If he was willing to love her as his sister, if he needed her more than anyone else, then she would follow him to certain doom, cursed or crushed as the case may be.

"Kanba, please, answer me. What were you about to say just now? Will you let me be cursed alongside you?"

But as he turned back to speak, the opportunity was stolen from him once again.

"Masako!"

A hail fire of bullets shot out from the darkness, aiming squarely at them. Screaming, Masako watched as sparks flew like shooting stars. Oh, how dearly she wished they were stars instead. A beat later, everything went dark and quiet, as if a curtain fell on the stage.

Beneath the night sky, she could smell her beloved brother's familiar scent. It took her back to the days when he cherished her as his sister. Was there once a time when he held her like this? His arms were warm, imbued with sweet, soft love that she couldn't possibly oppose, even if what lay beyond was a hopeless future. When she opened her eyes a crack, she realized that she was somehow completely unharmed.

"Kanba?"

He was collapsed on top of her. Then her back started to ache, and she realized he must have tackled her to the ground. When she shook his shoulders, she felt something warm and wet.

"Kanba!"

With a shriek, she wriggled her way out from under him. His back bore the gunshots meant for her; his skin smelled of gunpowder, and blood was pooling beneath his body. Then his fingers twitched slightly, and she grabbed his hand in both of hers, squeezing tightly. He was still conscious.

"You cannot escape, Takakura Kanba! Cease all resistance!"

There was nowhere left for them to run. But if they surrendered, he might survive.

"We will give you ten seconds. If you do not surrender, we will open fire! Ten!"

Masako slowly rose to her feet. There, in her path, stood a group of men dressed in black. They surrounded her and Kanba, preventing their surrender.

"Move! Kanba's going to die!" Masako shouted, pleading.

"It's pointless. Our crimes can never be forgiven. If we go out there, they'll execute us," one of them muttered.

"No...!"

Either way, Kanba was going to lose his life. As he struggled to breathe, she reached out and cupped his cheek.

Nine. Eight.

"I'm sorry, Mario-san. I failed to save you." As she spoke, she removed her trench coat. "I'll be the decoy. You take Kanba and get out of here!"

Seven. Six. Five.

She peeled off his black jacket riddled with bullet holes and pulled it on, using the collar to conceal her gorgeous curls. Dressed like this, they might mistake her for Kanba.

Four.

"Move!"

As the men all hesitated, she shoved them out of the way and took off running.

Under the leadership of Natsume Sahee, the Natsume family was driven by greed. In this world, the ambitious took charge; anything less was unworthy of fruit. Masako believed that this was her grandfather's curse, and so when her father threw it all away and went into hiding, she believed him to be a pure-hearted, selfless person. But then she saw his coffin, vague and formless and beautiful.

There could be no light without shadow. Kanba had rescued her and Mario from that shadow and sent them into the light—into the sunshine. But Masako was a mere child who couldn't see that, just as Yuri had said. This time, however, she would be the one to save him. She wouldn't let him die here in the dark.

"Goodness, I'd better crush them soon!"

She glanced over her shoulder just in time to see the group of men scatter in all different directions—one of them carrying Kanba.

Three. Two.

His black military jacket carried a warm, reassuring scent that put her at ease.

One.

On an especially snowy day, Masako's father took her and Mario by the hand and instructed them to say goodbye to Kanba.

"Masako, Mario, you're going to stay here."

Here was an apartment KIGA leased. Normally it was packed full of people who gave long speeches; Kanba and Masako always stood side by side, listening intently. She was convinced that her grandfather was a greedy tyrant while her father was a good person, so she always did her best to pay attention when he talked, even if she didn't really enjoy the speeches. Still, she could tell it wasn't an ordinary apartment.

"The two of you are going to help me with my work."

The two of us? Then what about Kanba? Masako looked at her father anxiously.

"Dad, no! Let Masako and Mario go back home to the Natsume estate. Let them be normal kids! I'll stay here instead!" young Kanba pleaded, clinging to his father's legs.

Masako looked at the two of them and realized what was going on. She grabbed Mario's mitten-clad hand; he blinked and looked at her.

Her father and brother were doing great work that their grandfather could never hope to replicate. Eventually they would come back to the Natsume estate to live with her and Mario, but for now, she needed to go back there and keep Mario safe until she finally managed to crush her accursed grandfather...or so she chose to believe, anyway. Otherwise she herself would have been crushed by the weight of her everyday life.

When she learned that Kanba was adopted by the Takakura family, Masako instinctively realized that their father must have died. As she watched him from a distance, Kanba's face clouded over more and more. Oh, how she wished to one day clear up those clouds and live with him in the sunshine... At least, that was what she told herself. But perhaps it was never meant to be.

And so, on that fateful day, she was unceremoniously stuffed into a car her grandfather had sent. Through the window, she could see Kanba standing out in the snow. And as he disappeared into the distance, she made her teary farewell.

The city was draped in a blanket of snow, and it was so cold, it felt like her tears would crystallize on her cheeks. After that, her father and brother never came home.

CHAPTER 05

O N THE MORNING of the bombing sixteen years ago, Watase Sanetoshi was dressed in a long white jacket reminiscent of a cape. The heels of his white boots clacked on the floor as he walked, heralding the beginning of the end of everything. Then he boarded a commuter train packed full of employees and students.

The organization had a car parked at every station. Carrying the black teddy bears they'd assembled in advance, each associate slipped into the crowd.

At one point, Sanetoshi concluded that he hated society with every fiber of his being. "Society" was made up of a handful of different boxes, and people bent themselves out of shape in a desperate attempt to fit within those constraints. They lived their lives never knowing their true form. Eventually they forgot everything and everyone they ever loved, and then they died.

This subway system was a mere microcosm of those boxes, designed to transport these human cattle. The world didn't need it and neither did he. He was chosen to live outside the box. Thus, his next move was to destroy it, and today was only the beginning. He smiled faintly as his white-gloved hands toyed with the black teddy bear he was carrying.

Then a small girl stepped inside from the neighboring train car, wearing a red *randsell* backpack on her shoulders. She slipped through the sea of legs and walked right up to him. And when he sensed her aura, all the hair on his body stood on end. As he looked down at her, she stared unflinchingly back at him with her large, round eyes. Her name was Momoka.

"I'm going to eject you from this world."

Strangely enough, he felt that this little child had the power to understand his outlook on society. *How absurd,* he thought. Even if he was right about her, she couldn't possibly hold her own against him.

"Stunning. And how will you achieve that?" he scoffed with a smirk. As if in response, she blinked several times, her long lashes fluttering. Then the train car and passengers all melted into the background until it was just the two of them.

Sanetoshi turned back to face her. This was a sight only afforded to them—a world only they could share, reminiscent of space, but with far fewer stars. He let go of the black teddy bear, and it floated in place, its sharp eyes glaring at Momoka. She lowered her heavy backpack and pulled out a notebook.

"This diary contains an incantation that can transfer fates. I will now recite it."

"I'm afraid you're too late. If only we had met a little sooner," he snickered. His hair grew like vines, painting the dark void of space with light and color. But Momoka didn't bat an eye.

"I'm going to send you flying through the darkness for all eternity," she declared. Her words turned everything to pale pink petals, spinning and scattering in all directions. The smile vanished from Sanetoshi's face, and in a blink, his flowers wilted.

"In that case, allow me to lock you inside my curse."

It all happened near-simultaneously: Momoka started reciting the spell, while Sanetoshi pressed his lips to his fingers, then pasted that "symbol" onto her forehead. She wasn't able to finish the incantation, and so she failed to save everything. The bears' eyes started flashing, and then the bombing occurred. But neither was the world destroyed.

The two gazed firmly into each other's eyes, each of them watching their inflicted curse take hold. Momoka's tiny body was split in two, and her soul was transformed into two penguin-shaped hats. Likewise, Sanetoshi was split in two, transforming into two sleek black rabbits with scarlet eyes. But he wasn't bothered by it. After all, he was one of the chosen few. Thus, he decided he would get his chance to annihilate the world sooner or later...and in the meantime, he vowed never to forget the little girl who risked her life to reject his ambition.

For a long, long time, he recalled the memories again and again. Slowly but surely, his anger at the girl who opposed him became indistinguishable from deep affection. Caught in the vortex of his curse, Momoka continued to keep watch over him as much as possible. And as he traveled down his cursed path toward the future, he waited for the day his postponed plans could finally be enacted.

Sixteen years later, the curse was no longer enough to hold Watase Sanetoshi.

It was late in the evening when I got the call informing me that Himari was taken to the hospital. I thanked the nurse, then hung up, pulled on my coat, and dashed out of the house. Arriving at the emergency room, I filled out the paperwork, then proceeded to the room where she lay asleep. Inside, Dr. Washizuka took one look at my ashen complexion and frowned.

Himari was hooked up to an EKG and wearing an oxygen mask. Worse still, she was assigned a private room located right near the nurses' station. This didn't help my anxiety, since patients who weren't in critical condition were placed in shared rooms much further away. Himari was hospitalized many times in the past, but this was the first time they'd ever put her *here*.

"When they brought her in, she was delirious, calling for you over and over. Did something happen between the two of you?" Dr. Washizuka asked me as I sat on the stool beside her bed, staring at my lap. There on my knees, Penguin No. 2 leaned as far as it could, peering at Himari's ghostly pale face.

I tried to think of an answer to his question, but couldn't. I hadn't been considerate of Himari's feelings. Fortunately my number was listed on her insurance card under "emergency contact info," but even if she could have contacted me on her own without the help of the hospital, I wasn't sure she actually would have. Also included in her tote bag were her wallet, handkerchief, adhesive bandages, cough drops, chapstick, and the key to the Takakura house. Oh, and the penguin hat.

"Is your brother around? I need to speak with him in my exam room. It's about something important."

"He won't be coming. You can have your conversation with me, right here," I replied flatly. "How long does Himari have left?"

"A few hours. Tomorrow morning at most. I'm sorry," he told me calmly.

"Please excuse me. I need to call my family."

I casually set No. 2 on the stool, then left the room. Out in the hall, I called my uncle, then Oginome-san. A short distance away, the nurses' station was bustling with activity.

Uncle Ikebe was very quiet; he must have gleaned Himari's condition from the sound of my voice. Bit by bit, I told him only the most relevant details. He told me he'd be here as soon as possible, instructed me to get some rest, then hung up.

Likewise, Oginome-san wasn't that shocked to hear that Himari was taken to the hospital. Instead, she calmly asked me what happened and whether I needed her to bring anything. This helped get me to think things through a bit more.

"There's a spare key taped to the underside of the potted plant at the far edge of the porch. Use it to get into the house. Then go to Himari's room and you'll see a bunch of cardboard boxes with my uncle's address on them. They have Himari's clothes inside…"

As I mumbled on and on, the house I had only just left rose to the forefront of my mind—the cold, dark, empty house with its chilly wood floors and ancient bathroom tile. And the cramped, cluttered kitchen. And the fridge covered in papers held up by magnets. And the warm orange light of the living room, and Himari's bedroom right next to it—a magical, fanciful room with a big pink four-poster bed—

"Shoma-kun? Are you okay?"

"Yeah, I'm fine. Sorry. Anyway, we've got her insurance card here...um...uhhh..."

All at once, my mind went blank, and I kept stammering over and over. Wasn't there something else? Something we needed?

"Slow down and take it easy. I'll just bring you and Himari-chan some spare clothes," she told me firmly, and I knew I could count on her.

"Okay. Thanks," I mumbled. "Hey, um, about Himari... They told me she's at the end of her rope. She might make it to tomorrow, but that's about it."

"Oh. Wow. That's...awful..." I could hear her voice grow muddled on the other end of the line. Maybe she was fighting back tears.

When I returned to the hospital room, I accidentally sat down on top of No. 2. Dr. Washizuka gave me an odd look, but didn't ask.

"Where's Dr. Sanetoshi?" I asked as the thought occurred to me. He had said Himari couldn't be cured, but maybe he would know of some other way to save her.

"Sanetoshi? Who are you talking about?"

"Dr. Sanetoshi, the internal specialist!" I shouted back on reflex. "He's been treating her illness, and I'd like to get his professional medical opinion!"

"Now hold on a minute. We don't have any 'internal specialists' at this hospital. Besides, I had a different doctor take over for me while I was out of the country. Didn't you meet him?"

"That's not true. His name was Watase Sanetoshi, and he was tall, with long hair, and..." What did his face look like again? What floor was his exam room on? Dr. Washizuka looked at me with concern as I searched for the words. "And he had two kids with him!"

"You know, I used to have an assistant by that name, once upon a time," he replied, smiling bitterly. "That reminds me—I actually had a dream about him just the other night. What a strange dream."

"So what happened to him?"

"He died sixteen years ago. In my dream, I think he called himself a ghost... Not very scientific, now is it?"

"A ghost...?"

That couldn't be possible. Himari, Kanba, and I had all met him in person dozens of times. He smelled like a greenhouse, and his hair glowed funny colors, and he always crossed his long legs, and he had two young twin assistants. But the one thing I couldn't remember was his face—almost like someone blacked it out with a Sharpie.

"Get some rest. The fatigue is clearly getting to you," Dr. Washizuka sighed.

Inside the pitch-dark KIGA hideout, Kanba sat in front of a dozen large computer monitors. He leaned against the chair with his full weight, enduring the pain in his back. Himari was nowhere to be seen; the only sound was that of his own labored breathing. The pain and panic made him sweat. Occasionally he would pause to wipe his brow with his sleeve as he watched cardboard boxes full of black teddy bears ship out one by one.

"In short, you three are cursed by the dead, and the curse is me. Stunning, isn't it?"

Sanetoshi stepped out from the shadows, his long white jacket fluttering behind him. The light from the computer monitors reflected off of his hair, creating ripples of pink and blue and yellow that spread through the darkness. His eyes were as deep and bottomless as space itself; they absorbed the light and twinkled mysteriously.

"This time, I *will* destroy the world. And I'm going to rub it in my little girlfriend's face."

"I don't care what happens to the world. I want to save Himari."

Kanba didn't take his eyes off the monitors for a single second. His voice was flat, and his breathing wasn't getting any slower. Why wasn't she here?

"You will. As proof, allow me to show you one of my magic spells... Survival Tactic," Sanetoshi whispered hoarsely into his ear.

Kanba's heart skipped a beat, and he looked up—but they were no longer in the same room as before.

"I'm really not the dramatic type," Sanetoshi shrugged, then started walking.

They were now floating in space—the same space reflected in his eyes. A breathtaking number of stars twinkled brightly, flying past and exploding all around them. Kanba had never seen space before, but the tension in the air told him he wouldn't last a moment outside of this contained area—he could feel it viscerally through his skin. It smelled nearly as sweet as the place the penguin queen always manifested.

"Watch." Sanetoshi held up his hand, and a portion of the invisible floor rose up like the lid of a box. Kanba peered down inside to find Masako's bedroom at the Natsume estate—a bird's-eye view of her bed.

"Masako...no..."

At the time Kanba awoke, he found that his injuries were already treated. The members of KIGA were there with him, but Masako was not.

Here she lay unconscious in bed, her ample curls fanned out over the bedsheets, surrounded by the Natsume family's private duty medical team, plus her butler Renjaku. Every visible inch of her was covered in bandages, and she looked to be in pain.

Kanba hated all the equipment and the tubes, but what he *really* hated was the sound of the EKG. Once it went flat, its obnoxious drone signaled a person's death.

"Now then, let us behold the miracle that will occur." Smirking, Sanetoshi bowed.

"My lady?! My lady!" Renjaku shrieked, drowning out the sound of the monitor. "*My lady*!" As the blood drained from her face, she clung to Masako's unconscious body. "MY LADY!"

It was the first time Kanba had ever seen Renjaku lose all control of her emotions. Meanwhile, Sanetoshi watched with a leisurely smile as the doctor reached over and checked Masako's pulse.

"She's gone."

"No... My lady!" Renjaku collapsed to the floor beside the bed and began to sob.

"Poor thing. It appears your twin sister has died," Sanetoshi remarked casually.

He took Kanba by the hand, and the two of them descended gently into Masako's bedroom. Kanba stood there dumbfounded as Sanetoshi walked over to Masako and peered intently at her face. She wasn't breathing.

"She's very pretty. Looking at her up close, I can tell the two of you are related." His fingers toyed with her glossy hair.

Neither Renjaku nor the medical team seemed to notice their presence. Timidly, Kanba approached the bed; Sanetoshi glanced over his shoulder and grinned as he gently stroked Masako's cheek with his palm. Then he pointed at the EKG monitor, and suddenly, the flatline pulsed to life. Startled, the doctor peered at Masako's face.

"Nngh..." Groaning, Masako lifted her heavy eyelids by a fraction.

"My lady?! Doctor, she's awake!" Renjaku scrambled back to her bedside. "My lady! My lady!" she whimpered in a watery voice.

"You there!" The doctor pointed at the one of the nurses and began to give hasty instructions.

"Where's...Mario-san...?" Masako asked, glancing in Renjaku's direction.

"You needn't worry, my lady. Mario-sama is resting in the room next door," she answered firmly. Then she pulled out a white handkerchief with her initials embroidered into it and wiped her tears.

"So he's alive?"

"Yes, of course, my lady!"

"Good... I'm glad..." Masako let out a shaky breath and closed her eyes once more, falling unconscious in her relief. Color returned to her lips and cheeks, and her body steadily regained its warmth.

"Masako..." Privately, Kanba heaved his own sigh of relief. This reminded him of the time Sanetoshi first saved Himari's life. Did he use this power to do it?

"Now do you see? I have the power to save Himari-chan," Sanetoshi boasted.

"Yeah..." Kanba nodded quietly. Unlike him, Sanetoshi could actually save her... The gunshot wounds on his back twinged slightly.

"Don't!" Masako suddenly shouted, reaching out with one hand. Her eyes were still closed, like she was dreaming. "Don't go, Kanba! Don't go with him!"

"Stop that, my lady. You have to rest!"

Following Sanetoshi's lead, Kanba turned to leave the room.

"You'll die!"

Kanba frowned a tiny fraction. Sanetoshi would destroy the world...but he would save Himari. Honestly, if it would save her life, what did it matter if he died in the process?

"You're wasting your time. You'll never reach him." Sanetoshi waved a dismissive hand in her direction. "Humans are programmed to ignore dissenting voices and seek an echo chamber. As such, the only voice he can hear now is mine."

Sanetoshi stooped down slightly, bringing himself down to Kanba's eye level.

"You haven't done anything wrong. You're making the right choice," he whispered in a sensual voice.

And the more Masako writhed, the more delighted he became.

"See? The more you oppose his actions, the farther he'll push you away, until eventually you can't reach him at all. You know that, right? More than anything else, humans want to be *needed*. They spend their lives yearning for it."

Then, while she was watching, he turned back to Kanba.

"Now go and wreak havoc to your heart's content. Let's conduct an experiment and find out how destructive the power of your love can be."

Sanetoshi gave Kanba a little push. The pain in his back faded, and his cold sweat dried. He walked to the shelf beside the bed, picked up half of Momoka's diary, and flipped past the grimy cover to examine its contents. As she grimaced at him, he afforded her a passing glance, then went back to Sanetoshi, who put an arm around his shoulders.

"Now then, let us be off." And with that, they slowly floated upward, back toward the void Sanetoshi created.

"Don't do it, Kanba! Don't get on that train! Don't go that way! Don't go!"

"Perhaps she's dreaming about taking the subway," Sanetoshi chuckled. "As of this moment, you're my new best friend."

But not even *that* managed to get a reaction out of Kanba. Once they returned to the void of space, Sanetoshi lifted up the lid to Masako's bedroom and dropped it back into place with a firm *CLACK*.

For Ringo, it was deeply strange to set foot in the Takakura house by herself. As she entered, she called out "Sorry for the intrusion," even though she knew no one was there. Then she went and packed her gym bag with a few days' worth of clean clothes for both Himari and Shoma.

If she used the spell she inherited from Momoka, she could transfer Himari's fate and save her life...but she still only had half of the diary. That said, even if Yuri was right and the other half was currently in the possession of a teenage girl named Natsume Masako, it didn't explain why this other girl was after the diary. And even if Ringo went and begged her, it wasn't likely she would agree to forfeit her half.

For the time being, she decided she would deliver the clothes to Shoma at the hospital, then quietly try to arrange a meeting with this Masako girl. He didn't need to know about it.

She sent a message to her mother, informing her that she was going to visit Himari in the hospital and would be home later than usual. Her mother still had no idea that the Takakura kids had any connection to the bombing sixteen years ago. She was generally a patient, forgiving woman, but if she found out, she might just forbid Ringo from ever associating with them again. Naturally, Ringo would disobey this order. Thus, it was better not to tell her in the first place.

Ringo didn't want to upset her mother. She cared a lot about their relationship—they only had each other now, after all. But she knew she would have to come clean about her dear friends eventually...and about the boy she loved. She would have to tell her mother about what sort of people they were, and what effect they had on her, and how they helped her mature as a person.

Then her phone started ringing on the coffee table where she'd left it. Thinking it might be Shoma, she ran over and answered it.

"Hello? Shoma-kun?" she blurted. There was a pause.

"I have the other half of the diary, Oginome-san."

Ringo recognized the voice as Kanba's.

"Kanba-kun?! Where are you? You have the diary?!"

She remembered both he and Shoma were looking for it at one point, but she figured he would be with Himari by now. Didn't he know she was in critical condition?

"Actually, you know, Himari-chan got taken to the hospital—"

"With our powers combined, we can save her," he cut in.

"Have you been looking for the diary all this time?"

Stricken with fear, she pulled out her half of the diary and hugged it to her chest. Had he stolen the other half from Natsume Masako?

"Yes, and I finally got my hands on it. Now the diary is complete," he declared. "But I need to stay where I am. They're after me."

"*They*? Where exactly are you, Kanba-kun?"

She heard him hold his breath.

"Let's meet up and complete the diary. I promise, I'll meet you there."

Ringo nodded without hesitation.

At night, the district of Ikebukuro was still swarmed with people, but the Sunshiny International Aquarium had long since closed for the day. The building was deserted; no one was at the ticket counter, and no one was lined up to enter. The surrounding area was dark, and the signposts were hard to make out.

Timidly, Ringo slipped inside. The carpeted floor muffled her footsteps as she moved from room to room, the glowing blue tanks her only guide. Here in the silent aquarium, the schools of fish paid her no mind, swimming or sleeping as they saw fit. As the contortions of the thick glass threatened to make her sick to her stomach, she steadily grew more and more cautious of her surroundings.

She didn't think Kanba would try anything funny; at the very least, he wouldn't do anything that would have a negative impact on Himari. But Ringo still had questions. Even if he and Shoma were technically estranged at the moment, why wouldn't he call his brother to tell him about the diary? And when he said "they're after me," was he talking about the remnants of the organization, like that tabloid journalist mentioned?

"Kanba-kun, where are you?"

It was a spacious building, and yet the darkness seemed to absorb her voice without letting it echo. No matter where she looked, all she could see was fish.

Then a voice suddenly spoke from above: "Oginome-san."

"Kanba-kun?" She froze, listening intently.

"Did you bring your half of the diary?"

For a moment, her gut instinct was to stay quiet. But Ringo had no reason to come all the way here empty-handed.

"Yeah, it's right here." In her arms was a bag containing just the half-diary.

"Thank you. Now come over here."

"Where?"

"Ahead of you, at the plaza."

Clutching her phone in one hand just in case, Ringo slowly walked in the direction of the plaza indicated to her by the sign-posts. Moments prior the fish had seemed creepy, but now she found she was scared to part from them.

"Kanba-kun, Himari-chan's waiting for us at the hospital. We need to go."

"Don't worry. Tomorrow, Himari and I will board the same train from sixteen years ago. We'll go to a new world where she can be saved."

"A new world? You mean, using the spell? Tell me, Kanba-kun, how much do you know about transferring fates? Did you get your half from that girl named Natsume-san?"

When did he learn about it, and how long was he acting on this knowledge? If he was actually being pursued, then he would naturally be looking for a place to hide. So why was he taking his sweet time?

Just then, two small, gleaming scarlet eyes caught Ringo's

attention. Swallowing, she walked over and crouched down to investigate. There, she found a black teddy bear.

"What is this thing? Kanba-kun, where are you?" she called out, rising to her feet.

"Thank you, Oginome-san."

His voice was soft, but a lot closer than she was expecting. She flinched in surprise.

"Kanba-kun, how did you know that Yuri-san gave me back her half of the diary? I hadn't told anyone yet. And how did you know about the spell?"

"I heard about it from a friend," Kanba replied calmly, without hesitation.

"Who?"

She whirled around, away from the teddy bear. Standing there in the darkness was a tall man with glowing white skin and eyes as deep as the ocean. His long, silky-looking hair added a hint of pink to the blue light of the aquarium.

"Where's Kanba-kun?" Ringo asked.

The man blinked at her wordlessly, his long lashes shining faintly. With every blink, strange patterns spread in the air, then faded away.

"Are you the friend he was talking about?"

His long, wide-collared white jacket slowly spread out from the top down, revealing his tight pants, boots, and gloves. Dressed from head to toe in all white, he glowed in the dark like a ghost.

"Good heavens, you look just like her," Sanetoshi commented without smiling. "I was scared, you know. I had this feeling that as long as you and that diary still existed, Momoka-chan was going to get my goat all over again."

"Who are you?" Ringo demanded, more firmly.

"Nice to meet you. I am a ghost," he replied, slowly and purposely. Then he moved his right foot back, pressed his right hand to his chest, and bowed, gracefully extending his left hand outward at his side.

"A ghost?" Ringo repeated.

But right as the words left her lips, the teddy bear exploded, sending her flying into the wall of the plaza. Her bag tore, and the diary half fell to the carpet.

There amid the smoke, Kanba appeared without the slightest sound. He walked up beside her and picked up the diary with both hands. Then he stared down at her limp, lifeless body.

"Stunning," Sanetoshi grinned, applauding. "Now then, go ahead and burn both halves. I'd do it myself, but I can't touch them."

Silently, without batting an eye, Kanba tossed Momoka's diary into the uncontrolled flames. Sanetoshi watched, entranced, as the cover warped and the pages turned to ash. His pale face and clothes were tinged red by the light of the fire.

"Now no one will ever know the fate transfer spell."

Using the last of her strength, Ringo turned her head. When she saw the diary was on fire, she pushed herself up and reached out for it.

"You still haven't given up, hmm?"

She glanced in Sanetoshi's direction, but otherwise ignored

him, grabbing at the two burning diary halves sitting in a stack on the carpet.

"Let me guess: you think the power of love will save the day?" Sanetoshi watched curiously as Ringo crawled along the floor at his feet. "Well, I'd think again if I were you. It's nearly burned to a crisp now."

"No! I'll never give up on Himari-chan!"

As she shouted, smoke filled her lungs, and she fell into a coughing fit. But she refused to give up on the people she cared about. She was going to save Himari's life, and heal Shoma's wounds, and maybe even get Kanba back.

Sanetoshi bent over, hands on his knees, leaning in close to her face. "For the record, it's for your own good. If you recite that incantation, you'll pay the price, and the flames of the curse will burn you...just like this."

He looked at the diary, which was now burned up beyond recognition. Beside it, Ringo lay motionless, her hand and sleeve both singed black.

"If you burn away, you'll cease to exist. Surely you don't want that, do you?"

She didn't answer. She didn't understand what he was talking about, and even if she did, she couldn't breathe well enough to speak.

Stretching slightly, he called out to Kanba: "Now then, let us be off. The train of fate awaits us."

In response, Kanba walked right up to him. Together, they turned away from Ringo and headed into the forest of fish tanks.

Struggling to stay conscious, she watched them disappear. What did he mean by "the train of fate"?

When she finally *did* pass out, her last thoughts, like the majority of her other thoughts, were of Shoma. There was still so much she hadn't told him... She hadn't even finished packing clothes for him.

Himari-chan...Momoka...I'm sorry...

But even her shakiest thoughts were absorbed by the thick glass.

Time passed as I waited and waited for Oginome-san to show up. I tried calling her a handful of times, but she never answered... and before I knew it, night fell. As I watched Himari's unchanging EKG, the other hospital visitors dwindled, and Penguin No. 2 dozed off at my feet. Then it was time for lights out. A nurse came and brought me a cot; I laid myself down on it, but kept my eyes open, watching the EKG and its mostly steady rhythm while listening to Himari's unnaturally faint breathing.

The room was kept at a carefully controlled temperature, just barely warm. Physically I was exhausted, but my brain was wide awake, and I got the sense I wouldn't be sleeping anytime soon. I couldn't stop worrying about Oginome-san, and on top of that, Himari was going to die at some point tonight or tomorrow. It was unthinkable, and yet it was probably fact. When it happened, would I cry? How would I keep living my life? Was it even *possible* for me to live on my own?

In the past, when Himari was in critical condition, I often stopped to think long and hard about what her death would mean for us. I never really had to grapple with the loss of a close family member. Of course, I had other relatives besides just Uncle Ikebe, but none of them wanted anything to do with the children of Takakura Kenzan and Chiemi. We never had a funeral or anything for our parents, either—technically they were just missing. I did go to Kanba's dad's funeral a long time ago, but I was really young at the time, and I was too busy worried about whether Himari was tired or whether Kanba was sad. All in all, it was just a hectic day spent surrounded by grown-ups wearing all black.

If Himari died, Uncle Ikebe would probably be the one to take charge and organize her funeral. She would lay there like a little porcelain doll, wearing that white dress, fated never to stir again, while someone else applied makeup to her face. The rest of the coffin would be packed full of flowers. Then, like with Kanba's dad's funeral, we would sit in the crematorium and eat bland prepackaged lunches while waiting for her body to be reduced to bones.

Never again would she look at me with those big, round eyes. Never again would she speak to me, and her natural scent would be overwritten with the stench of death. Her bedroom at the Takakura house would never be occupied again, nor would the room Uncle Ikebe set up for her at his place. Instead, traces of the life she once lived would remain scattered throughout the world, and every time I saw one, I would feel her absence and question myself all over again.

I thought about Tabuki Keiju. When the cause of death was illness, there was no real way to fight it; without an outlet, any lingering resentment would build up indefinitely. But if you knew exactly who caused the death of your loved one, perhaps it was only natural to bear a grudge against them and contemplate revenge.

"Hello? Sorry for calling so late. I was just wondering if something happened. I don't think we need the clothes anymore, so please just come see Himari while there's time. I'll be here when you get here," I told Oginome-san's voicemail. Then I flipped the blanket back, sat down on the cot, and stared into space.

Of all the absurd and fantastical events that happened to us thus far, it was this moment—this dark hospital room—that didn't feel quite real to me. I felt so numb, I couldn't tell if I was scared or sad. I told Oginome-san to *come see Himari*, but deep down, what I meant was *come see me*. It was by no means a happy occasion, but maybe with her around I could keep myself together long enough to figure myself out.

Just then, the windowpane shattered, and the curtains began to rustle in the wind. Startled, I looked up. It was Kanba, one foot on the windowsill.

"An—Kanba," I hastily corrected myself. He wasn't my *aniki* anymore. The chilly breeze helped sharpen my senses.

"I came to get Himari," he told me in a hard voice.

"You came to...get her...?"

I rose to my feet and staggered toward Himari's bed. Kanba always said he would save her, but at the same time, he was quite possibly a murderer. I couldn't begin to know what he was thinking.

"This world is corrupt. You know that, right?" He hopped down into the room and looked at me intently. I couldn't read any emotion in his eyes, but he didn't seem to be glaring at me—just looking.

"What are you planning to do with her?" I demanded.

"We have to make our parents' dream come true," he replied matter-of-factly.

"What are you talking about? What the hell is wrong with you?! Himari's on her *deathbed*!" I screamed at him, purely on impulse. Then it occurred to me that the nurses might come running. What would happen then? Would my brother hurt even more innocent people?

"This senseless world is going to change. Same day, same time, at the place where our fate resides. And Himari's life will be saved."

He was practically incoherent. He always used to be the smart one, the rational one—what happened to that? Now his words were vague and emotionally driven.

"What, so you're planning to sacrifice hundreds of innocent lives? That's not going to save her!"

"Takakura-san?"

A nurse was calling from out in the hall. I started to panic. If they caught him in here, there was zero chance he would apologize and surrender quietly. "Uh—"

But before I could say anything, Kanba shoved me out of the way, then pulled a slightly singed jackknife out of his pocket and stabbed it into the handle of the sliding door, jamming it.

"Takakura-san, is something wrong?" the nurse called. I could hear her trying to open the door, but she couldn't compete with Kanba's strength plus that of the knife. "Takakura-san?"

"Kanba!"

This was nothing like his usual style. It was just violent, with no rationality.

"If you don't see society for how it truly is, you're blind. This world will never give us fruit. That's why we gotta change it," he told me as he held the door shut behind him.

"No. That's not acceptable."

He was lying when he claimed it was all for Himari. He didn't care about me *or* her—we didn't even enter his line of sight. If anyone was blind, it was him.

"I don't care if you accept it." His eyes gleamed scarlet. "Don't get in my way."

He lowered the zipper on his coat just enough to pull a small black handgun from an inside pocket. I didn't know anything about the different types of guns, so I couldn't tell what it was or even if it was real. All I knew was that my brother was pointing a gun at me with his finger firmly on the trigger.

"Maybe part of me always wanted to do this to you."

The gunshot was louder than I expected, and a second later, everything went dark.

I recognized this twilit beach. I was standing with my white boots buried in the wet sand, tired but enjoying the smell of the sea, wearing a wide-brimmed straw hat that felt too feminine for a boy. The summer sun was still high in the sky, but the tide was rolling in, and we were scared we wouldn't be able to find what we were looking for.

What we sought wasn't clams or seashells or shards of glass— not even cute little crabs. With my pail and shovel in hand, I dashed through the groups of families heading home for the day, calling her name, just like the day we first became a family ourselves. But this time we were closer, and we knew each other much better.

"Shoma!"

I turned to find my father standing there. Like usual, my mother was right beside him. She was always hovering in his vicinity, and at the time, I found it reassuring. The sight of them standing side by side was a soothing one.

"I'm going to go ask the lifeguard one more time if they've seen any lost children. While I'm gone, I want you and Kanba to help your father look for her, okay?" Restlessly, my mother took the pail and shovel from my hands. "But don't go too far."

"It'll be all right. We'll find her in no time," my father replied with a confident smile. He was always like that—could always find the words to convince you of his beliefs. Be it windy nights, snowy nights, or nights when we were sick or hungry, he would tell us it would be all right, and sure enough, it was. Even if it actually *wasn't* all right, it was to us.

"Let's go, Shoma," a young Kanba declared, tugging on my sleeve with a determined look in his eyes. And so the two of us ran aimlessly around the beach.

"Watch your step! Don't trip!" our father shouted after us, making my back twinge.

"I wonder where she slipped off to, anyways. Little twerp." For as long as I'd known him, Kanba always liked to act like he was *so* much older than us. "Let's search that rocky place."

It was still early into summer, and on the coast, the wind at sunset was colder than you'd think. The brim of my straw hat flapped in the breeze.

"Himariiii! HIMARIIII!"

Out here, no one else was nearby. Meanwhile, the sun slowly sank beneath the horizon, melting into the sky. Inside the rock cave was a bunch of barnacles and bugs I'd never seen before; we searched all around, but there was no sign of Himari anywhere. Ahead of us, the beach seemed to stretch on endlessly.

"Did you find her?" my father asked as he walked up to us.

He put a hand on my hat—a big, strong hand. When I grew up, I was sure I was going to have hands just like his. But in actuality, my hands turned out a lot smaller and nowhere near as burly. No idea if that was a good or bad thing.

"Knowing her, she probably got lost while looking for seashells," my father sighed. "Surely she couldn't have gone very far."

"Did you find her?" my mother called from a distance as she jogged up. "The lifeguard hasn't seen her, but he said he'd help look."

"Dad, we're gonna go check over there now," Kanba declared, shooting me a look.

"Okay then, I'll check the opposite side. But be careful, you two."

Our father always let us have our independence as much as possible, as long as it wasn't too dangerous. That was probably the reason why Kanba grew up to be such a reckless hothead. Likewise, I used to be the same as him, but that was before years of looking after him and Himari turned me into a worrywart.

"Shoma, are you all right?" my mother asked, stooping down to smile at me. "Are you feeling worn out? Want to sit and wait with me?"

"Shoma, get over here!" Kanba turned away and ran off across the tangerine sand.

We were all so different, with completely different patterns of thought and behavior. But that didn't matter because we were a family. At the end of the day, I could rest assured that we'd all meet up and take the same train home...though looking back, I'm not sure how I was so sure of that.

"Sho-chan!"

As I was reliving this distant memory, immersed in a time long since passed, I heard a familiar voice.

"Himari? Is that you?" I answered in my mind.

I looked over at my parents talking to the lifeguard in the distance, then turned and started walking in Kanba's direction.

"Yup, it's me. Say, Sho-chan, do you remember the day we went digging for clams?"

"Yeah. It was the first trip we ever took as a family. I remember it all really clearly... Man, it's been a long time since I've seen the ocean. Too long." Breathing heavily, I moved my boot-clad legs as fast as they would go, chasing after Kanba.

"I was so excited, I accidentally got lost. See, I found these really pretty shells with rainbow colors on the back."

For as long as I'd known her, Himari loved all things small, cute, or pretty.

"Yeah, I remember. When we finally found you, your little pail was packed full of them," I snickered. "And Kanba was like, 'You know you can't eat those, right?'"

"I was so scared. It felt like everyone else in the world had vanished, and I wasn't sure how I was going to survive. But then you found me."

"Yep. Kanba and me tore the whole beach upside-down looking for you. And as soon as you saw us, you burst into tears."

Come to think of it, that was perhaps the first time Himari ever let her guard down around us.

"I did, didn't I? That was the moment I realized I mattered enough for someone to look for me. They were happy tears."

Chest aching, I finally caught up to Kanba, who was busy searching for Himari in a different rock cave. I took it upon myself to search the surrounding area. But the more I walked, the more I worked up a sweat. Oh, how I wished I could strip off my shirt and my stupid hat.

"No matter how far I wandered, I knew you and Kan-chan would always find me. And it meant a lot to know that someone was willing to look." I could tell from her voice that she was smiling. "I loved every minute of my life with you two. Thank you so much."

"What are you talking about? It's not over yet!"

The simple act of saying it out loud made me sad. How could I possibly stop it from ending? She was going to die tonight or tomorrow. I had no way to overturn that fate.

"Yeah, you're right. We'll always be together...which means it's our turn to go and find Kan-chan."

"What do you mean?"

"He's lost, just like I was."

I watched little Kanba climb up on the rock and shout for Himari while scanning the area.

"But...it's too late now..."

He became a completely different person in the time since then. When he looked at me, his eyes were cold and...resentful, almost.

"You're the only one who can stop him, Sho-chan."

"Can I...?"

Kanba vowed to *make our parents' dream come true.* Instantly, I knew what he meant by that. But what made him start to think like that? Why did he think saving Himari's life was inseparably tied to the bombing?

"Find him. Find his heart. He's all alone right now, and he's crying." Her voice was soft and warm, like my mother's. "Hey, Sho-chan? Do you hate Mom and Dad?"

"Well..." Searching for Himari, I followed Kanba up onto the rock, struggling to keep my balance in the face of the wind.

"They're still our family, Sho-chan. That's why I wanted you to remember them."

And I did. I remembered the feeling of my dad's burly hands, and I remembered how my mom was always sweet and a tiny bit overprotective. Thanks to them, the three of us had a family and a place to call home.

"Please don't curse our fate. It was our precious fate that brought us together at all."

"*Himari!*"

Kanba's shout brought me back to the beach. And as the incredibly vivid dream played out in my mind, we found her all over again, all curled up. When she looked up and saw us, sure enough, she burst into tears.

"It's all right now, Himari." That was how I always spoke to her at the time.

"Are you hurt, Himari?" Kanba asked. But Himari was too busy sobbing to answer. "I see you found a lotta shells. You know you can't eat those, right?"

I laughed in spite of myself.

"Daaaad! Moooom! We found Himariiii!" he shouted into the distance, waving them over.

Yes, I dearly loved my family. No matter how far they wandered, no matter what they did, I couldn't possibly hate them—not now, not ever.

As I slowly, gradually awoke, the first thing I noticed was the morning sun streaming in through the open window of the hospital room. On the floor was a white bullet the size of a ping-pong ball. Still, I told myself Kanba didn't try to kill me.

"Kanba!" I bolted upright. Himari wasn't in her bed, and all the medical equipment was put away.

"Good morning," a voice said suddenly.

"Huh?" I looked around the room. "Who's there?"

"I'm over here."

My eyes landed on the penguin hat on the bedside table.

"I see you're finally awake, Takakura Shoma-kun." The hat's eyes gleamed faintly. "Hurry. The train of fate will soon depart, and you must board it."

"Who are you? You're not the penguin queen." I hopped off the cot and walked over to it, rubbing my eyes.

"It was your sister's power that helped me. I'm sure you accepted her help as well."

The hat's voice was high-pitched like a child's, but with a degree of elegance to it that reminded me of Oginome-san. I grabbed the hat and dashed out of the room.

"Takakura-san?"

"Takakura-san, wait!"

The nurses at the nurses' station called after me, but I ignored them and bolted out of the hospital with Penguin No. 2 in tow.

Kanba actually took Himari, and today, he was planning to recreate the bombing from sixteen years ago. I couldn't afford to get bogged down in hatred. I needed to stop him and get her back.

"You mustn't miss the train. The black rabbits are trying to destroy the world, and you two are the only people who can stop it."

"You *two*?" I asked the hat in my hand.

"You and Kanba-kun."

"Kanba? But he's..."

I raced through the chilly city without a coat on. I just needed to get to the subway—the same place and time as sixteen years ago.

"That train is where you'll find it," the hat explained as I gasped for breath.

"Find what?"

"Your Penguindrum."

I looked down at Penguin No. 2 jogging along at my feet. Likewise, it glanced up at me. Would I recognize the Penguindrum when I saw it?

Even without a coat on, I was already sweating up a storm from all the exercise. I dove into the crowd of commuters and students and followed them through the turnstiles. When I reached the Nishi-Shinjuku Station platform, I boarded the subway.

If the penguin hat was to be believed, then Kanba was somewhere on this train.

Ogikubo, Higashi-Koenji, Nakano-sakaue, then Nishi-Shinjuku. As the train followed its route, the men boarded with black teddy bears at each station, camouflaged among the crowd. Likewise, Kanba and Sanetoshi stepped aboard together, waiting quietly for the big moment to roll around.

Sanetoshi was smiling, pleased to have a second chance at this challenging endeavor. No one could stop him this time—even Momoka was cursed into inaction. The people around them were heading off to start another ordinary day, wasting their precious lives being packed into a box. But now he was finally going to set them free. Soon, they would all take the first step toward a just society.

"We humans are such sad, pathetic creatures. We spend our whole lives refusing to set one foot outside our bubbles," he whispered to Kanba, who listened closely. "We simply can't cross that line, not even to connect with the person right next to us. We're all loners at heart. But we'll never gain anything from staying in these cramped little cages."

Kanba's expression didn't shift a fraction. Instead, he glanced around at the other men holding teddy bears in the train car with them, keeping tabs on them.

"There's no exit and no one who can save them. The only option is to destroy it all. The cages...the people...the world!" Sanetoshi declared, suppressing the chuckle in his throat. His long hair shook, and a yellow ring rippled outward through the train car.

"*Kanba*!" Shoma shouted hoarsely.

Kanba slowly turned in the direction of the voice. Shoma was standing there amid the passengers, bedhead in full force, staring him down.

"So you showed up," he replied, unsurprised, as if he'd predicted it.

"Let's settle this, Kanba."

Shoma was clutching the penguin hat tightly in one hand. She believed that the two of them could do it—even if it wasn't exactly according to fate.

PENGUINDRUM

CHAPTER 06

I F DESTINY WAS TRULY A PART of every single human being's life, then we must have shared our time together while trapped inside our individual cages. We didn't know if we could ever leave, but even then, we never gave up. Most likely, we carried that memory with us from before we were born.

"Where am I? Why am I here?"

I was inside a wooden box with metal bars over the opening. But there was nothing beyond those bars—or at least, nothing that I could see. I didn't know how long I was in there, nor did I know whether I would ever get to leave. But as I sat there, I found myself torn between a desire to leave and a strange sense of apathy.

The silence made my ears ring. Then I heard a faint sound in the distance. Perking up my ears, I grabbed the bars of the cage and squinted out at the darkness. Sure enough, there was another cage out there. And behind its bars was a young Kanba.

"Who are you?" I asked bluntly.

"Who are *you*?" he asked back.

That was the moment our lives intersected. Neither of us knew why we were forced to be here. But while we were both scared and vaguely frustrated, neither of us felt like there was anything we could do about it, and eventually it all stopped mattering. Here inside the cages, there was no food or water.

"Hey, Shoma, you alive in there?" Kanba called hoarsely.

"Yeah, I'm alive. You?" I was curled up on the floor of my cage, refusing to budge.

"Just barely. Ugh, I'm so dizzy... Y'know, I was having a dream where I was eating a big plate of curry." He scratched his head.

"Wow, that sounds good. I should start eating in my dreams, too," I mused.

"Don't bother. Seriously, it only makes you hungrier when you wake up. Besides..."

"Besides, what?"

"We shouldn't sleep anymore or else we might not wake up again." His expression was cold and hard.

"You mean we'll die?" If so, then that meant we were alive right now.

"Yeah. At this rate, at least."

If we were fated to die here right from the start, then why were we alive at all?

As Kanba and I eyed each other across the train car, Watase Sanetoshi chuckled, and the penguin hat in my hand grew faintly warm. Just then, the subway lights all clicked off, and the crowds of passengers all disappeared from sight. In the darkness, I could see black teddy bears scattered all throughout the train car, their scarlet eyes glowing.

"Simply stunning." Sanetoshi clapped his white-gloved hands. "Welcome aboard the train of fate."

"Where's Himari?! Give her back!" I thought I wasn't scared anymore, but my voice was threatening to crack.

"She's right here." Kanba's eyes were even more vacant than they were at the hospital, like glass marbles with an eerie sheen.

Sanetoshi smirked and twirled his cape-like white jacket. It stretched to fill the entire train car. Instinctively, I ducked, shielding my head. Then the scent of supple plants hit my nostrils.

"Himari!"

The pitch-black train car rolled sideways, and everything went white—the floor, the seats, the hanging straps, all of it. Unlike the darkness, it felt like a true void, and it was terrifying. Then, between where Kanba and I were standing, an entire four-poster bed appeared with Himari in it. Her long, soft hair spread out over the faint peach-pink sheets, framing her ghostly pale face. Her eyes were firmly closed, and she was so small, the bed practically engulfed her.

Kanba stared at me, his gaze unwavering. "The only way to save Himari's life is to complete the mission."

"How is that supposed to save her?! What will you get out of it, Kanba?! Are you seriously going to hurt even more people?!"

He narrowed his eyes slightly. "It's our Survival Tactic."

"Survival Tactic?" I'd heard the phrase a dozen times by now. Maybe Tabuki Keiju mentioned it in class at one point: *biological survival strategies*. But what did it mean?

"A pure biosphere is controlled by a framework of self-serving rules that exist beyond humanity's capacity for good or evil. Morality has no meaning. In other words, there is no one in the world who can stop this destiny." Sanetoshi spread his arms out wide. "Behold."

The black teddy bears rose up, scattered around the bright white void. As they started to spin, the world slowly turned back into a pitch-black train car. Himari was still in bed asleep, swaying with the motions of the speeding train.

"Pure? This is your idea of *pure*?" If being a pure biological organism meant hurting everyone around us, then I would sooner be tainted. I would choose to be a sinful human with a functioning moral compass.

I could hear a ticking sound, like that of a timer. I looked down at the penguin hat clutched tightly in my hand. What was I supposed to do now? I could see Kanba and Himari right in front of me, both still very much in human form. But I couldn't get through to Kanba at all, and it felt like there was nothing left.

"Watch closely, Momoka-chan. This time, you *will* witness the destruction of the world." With a satisfied smirk, he glanced at the hat.

"Kanba, why...?" I mumbled.

But Kanba didn't seem to hear me. He just stood there perfectly still, surrounded by black teddy bears, unblinking.

Inside the cages, we grew gaunt, sitting around for what felt like an eternity with our minds less than sharp. Our senses were growing numb, and our joints ached from all the time spent sitting still.

"Shoma, are you still alive?" asked Kanba in a feeble voice.

I didn't even have the strength to look over at him. "Yeah, and I take it you are too."

For some reason, it felt like a good thing. Even if we were going to die eventually, I was glad it hadn't happened yet.

"Hey, why don't we make a promise?"

"What kind of promise?"

"At this rate, one of us is gonna die. So we should make this promise while we still have time." Groaning faintly, Kanba pushed himself up into a sitting position. "If one of us manages to get out alive, we have to do something the other one wanted to do. And there's something I wanna say to the person I love."

I knew nothing of the world outside my cage. I didn't even know if it existed—did anyone? But at the same time, it seemed like a good idea. We needed the morale boost.

"So you want me to pass on a message? Maybe I should do that, too. But what would I even say?"

I attempted to picture the concept of "the person I love." The image in my head was soft and scary, sweet and sour, painful and precious. *Seems about right.*

"What the heck? What's this?" I could hear Kanba rustling around in his cage.

"What's wrong?" I asked without moving.

"There's something in here, in the corner of my cage."

I just barely managed to raise my heavy head and look in Kanba's direction. His little hand was holding a bright red apple.

"It's an apple," he muttered, dumbstruck. "There was an apple in here!"

That was the moment I knew that Kanba was chosen.

"Hey, I bet you have one, too. You should look!"

"I don't," I replied without missing a beat. "You've been chosen, Kanba."

"Chosen? By who? For what?"

"They've decided that you're the one who's going to survive. So I guess you better keep that promise, okay? Pass on a message to the person I love. I just can't think of what to say yet."

It was a stunning revelation, but I didn't feel like crying or mourning. At some point, we came to believe that it was normal for humans to be filtered into different categories. I couldn't remember where I learned this, but even though I hated it, a part of me was ready to accept it anyway.

"Okay. Sorry... I guess this is fate."

Was that how fate shaped our lives—shaped the world? Were we destined to wait for death without ever breaking out of the box?

We froze, unmoving, just glaring at each other. I could relate to Kanba's desire to save Himari; even in that very moment,

I was pretty sure I understood how he must have felt. But why did it have to involve throwing in his lot with Watase Sanetoshi and KIGA? Was Sanetoshi really a ghost? Was he once human?

"You still don't get it? The sky above him was always dark, and we humans need light," Sanetoshi sighed, bored. "Now that he's finally found a ray of hope, it's the only thing that gives his life meaning."

Was he talking about Himari? If so, then we had something in common.

"Right now, the world is trying to take that light from him. And you're taking *their* side, casting him into the abyss and leaving him to die."

"No! I wouldn't do that!"

Not once had I ever wanted to steal from Kanba. Regardless of whether his light was Himari or something else entirely, I never contemplated taking it for myself, much less abandoning him.

"Kanba!"

I called his name, but he didn't answer. Maybe we took him for granted. We were together for *years*, but how well did I really know him? Maybe I'd hurt him without realizing. Was this my punishment?

"I'm the only one who can save him. I can give him enough power to reach the light. What can *you* give him?" Sanetoshi raised his eyebrows, scoffing at me.

"What can I...give Kanba...?"

Nothing, I thought to myself. Watase Sanetoshi wasn't talking about cooking him dinner or ironing his shirts or nagging him or helping him with his homework. He was talking about something bigger—something life changing. I couldn't give him anything like that; I didn't *have* anything like that. Had I lived my whole life dumping my sins on Kanba's shoulders?

Just then, the train of fate came to a sudden stop. Thrown off-balance, I let out a yelp. When I looked out the window, I could see the perfectly ordinary Yotsuya Station platform... I was running out of time.

"Oginome-san!"

She staggered onto the train, wearing a badly charred school uniform, and glared at Sanetoshi. She had a cut on her cheek, and her glossy hair was slightly tousled.

"*I'm* going to save Himari-chan! It's my destiny!" Her eyes shone ever more defiantly from beneath her thick bangs.

"Oginome-san, what are you doing here?"

She was supposed to go to my house to pick up some clothes for us, but then she never showed up at the hospital. Rest assured, I hadn't forgotten that little detail. But I *really* wasn't expecting to see her on this train.

"I'm here to transfer Himari-chan's fate. I'll use the spell from the diary and save her life." Her face in profile exuded strength, determination, and dignity.

I remembered Yuri-san talking about the "transfer of fate" at some point in the past. But even if it was truly possible, we didn't have the diary.

"I see someone's a hard worker." Sanetoshi smirked faintly. "But how will you do that now that the diary's been burned to ash?

You don't know the spell—the most important words Momoka-chan left behind."

Sanetoshi seemed to be having the time of his life. He looked at Oginome-san with full confidence that he was going to succeed.

"Oh, I know them. I know the most important words. And I'm gonna take a gamble!"

I thought back to the time I found Oginome-san chatting with Double H outside my house. *We named the album after the words that always meant the most to her,* the pop star duo had said. Then they gave Oginome-san their new CD and walked off.

I didn't know the words that meant the most to Himari. Or maybe I simply didn't know enough about her, or Kanba, or myself, or the world around us. Still, my only choice was to keep living. Was that not enough?

"Do you? Are you sure? If you recite the incantation, you'll pay the price, you know. The flames of the curse will consume you, and you'll cease to exist." Sanetoshi scrutinized my expression, then Oginome-san's, endlessly amused. "Aren't you frightened?"

"If it means I can save someone I love, then I'm willing to accept my punishment!" she declared, unwavering. And in that moment, she was beautiful.

"No! Stop! We're the ones who should take the punishment!"

"Shoma-kun..." She looked at me sadly.

"Right, Kanba? *Kanba*!"

I turned back to my brother standing beside Sanetoshi. He wasn't looking at us, but rather, slightly lower. Contained within those glass marbles was a deep abyss, endless like space itself...

and reminiscent of Sanetoshi's. His star-studded gaze flew right past us.

"This was always our fate. We Takakura siblings have been cursed by our past...ever since we first met all those years ago."

"Don't be ridiculous! That's not true!" Oginome-san shouted.

"It's okay. I finally understand why I didn't die back there... It was all for this moment." I smiled at her, then turned to my brother. "Kanba, I'm going to get you back. Even if it costs me everything!"

Even if it meant going against the rules of our pure biosphere.

But right as Kanba finally glanced in my direction—

"*Survival Tactiiiic!*"

"Huh?" Stupidly, I belatedly realized I was no longer holding the penguin hat. "Where's the hat?!"

A gust of wind shot straight through the subway—so hard, it took my breath away. Suddenly, my vision was obscured with white lace and frills...sparkly buttons...waves of adorable ribbons... and the smell of Himari's shampoo. It was all so overwhelming, I could barely stand; crouching down low, I cradled my head in my arms. But though I was startled, I wasn't frightened in the least.

Soap bubbles and the sound of someone humming. A yellow star reminiscent of a Christmas decoration. The soft tinkling of a music box. Brightly colored balls of yarn. The smell of chocolate and vanilla essence. Smiling, I blinked back tears. As far as I could tell, this wasn't the work of that foul-mouthed queen. This was a space Himari had created—I was sure of it almost instantly.

The wind softened, and I straightened up. Sure enough, I could see none other than Himari herself, walking out from between the folds of white fabric. She was wearing the penguin hat, but her eyes weren't glowing red. Then the frills on the collar, sleeves, and hem of her white nightgown began to puff up even larger. Slowly, she examined her own handiwork.

"Kan-chan," she murmured. At this, the decadent frills of her nightgown stretched straight down to the uneven white fabric floor, creating a path. I followed her gaze and spotted Kanba floating in midair, surrounded by dozens upon dozens of black teddy bears, hanging his head.

"Kanba!" I called to him. But he didn't look up. He was standing upright, but he was as still as a corpse.

Barefoot, Himari dashed up the white fabric path to reach him. The white lace of her nightgown brushed against her slender arms, waist, and thighs, enveloping her, spreading out to engulf the entire space in one fluttering motion.

"Kan-chan, wake up!" she called out, her voice carrying through the teddy bear cage that surrounded him. Her bare feet were now completely buried in the frilly fabric floor, as if the space itself was contained entirely within the bounds of her nightgown. "I came to get you, Kan-chan. Let's go home now, okay?" Her long hair swayed as she tilted her head.

"Home? What home? I can't go home yet...I still haven't achieved my..."

Before he could finish his sentence, she pushed her way through the teddy bears and wrapped her arms around him. The bears started to spin, their eyes glinting scarlet.

"Himari!" I attempted to climb up the frilly path created from her nightgown, but every step was so pillowy, I could scarcely keep my balance.

The bears spun in a circle around Himari and Kanba, causing a rainbow of ice shards to rain down on them. In the light, the cold ice cast beautiful patterns on the white fabric, like a stained-glass window. But the chill froze Himari's body and slowly started to damage the white fabric world.

"Look—life is its own punishment, right? The whole time I lived in the Takakura house, I was dealt dozens of little punishments," Himari explained, cupping Kanba's cheek and smiling. One of the bigger ice shards struck the back of her hand, and the wound swiftly began to bleed, trickling across her skin.

If life really was its own punishment, then the three of us had endured punishment for years now—right from the moment we were born. Slowly but surely, I made my way up the soft, pillowy path.

"Sho-chan's very particular about stuff. Did you know he keeps all the seasonings in a specific order? Salt, pepper, soy sauce, rice wine, mirin, soup mix. And he nags us like he's our mom too. 'Quit eating chips or you'll spoil your appetite!' I swear, he treats us like little kids. And *you* always fall into a food coma right after we eat. We keep warning you that you'll turn into a cow, but you always ignore us. Of course, if *I* tried to do that, you'd get mad at me, you hypocrite!" She giggled. "You always leave your used tissues everywhere, and you always leave the toilet seat up. That's why Sho-chan makes fun of your filthy playboy germs."

Icicle arrows in red, blue, yellow, and green came flooding down in a torrent far more intense than that of rain or snow, all of it aiming for Himari. Her fluffy long nightgown was torn to shreds, and her body was dotted with bloody cuts.

"Himari!"

Truth be told, I didn't choose to have Kanba in my life. I never understood why *he* got to be the "older brother" when we were both born on the same day. Nevertheless, on the day Mom and Dad brought him into the family, I was told to call him Aniki. But things weren't that simple. We couldn't just start being brothers from that day on. I never even *wanted* an older brother.

I staggered again and again, fighting my way up the white fabric to reach the place where they stood. At the rate things were going, Himari was going to bleed to death. That wasn't her punishment—it was meant to be *mine*.

"But even then, we still stayed together. And no matter how small or boring the punishments were, the next thing we knew, it all turned into special memories. I mean, it's thanks to you and Sho-chan that I feel like I really lived. I was Takakura Himari—I laughed, I cried, I got mad...and I loved you." There was no pain in her voice, and she refused to pull away from Kanba. "I don't want to forget you... I don't want to lose you."

But Kanba kept staring out at the sparkling ice arrows.

"Himari! Kanba!" I screamed at the top of my lungs, but I couldn't tell if my voice could reach them. They still felt so far away.

"Kan-chan, please, come home." Himari squeezed him tighter, and the teddy bears hit her with even more ice—enough for them to disappear behind.

"I can't. I still haven't given you anything," he replied in a flat, emotionless voice. "I *can't* give you anything."

My eyes widened. All this time, Kanba stood there unscathed—but now, suddenly, he was bleeding.

"Kanba!"

The bright crimson looked so gruesomely vivid against the white background. The fabric at their feet turned from pink to deep scarlet—and the pool of blood was spreading quickly. Kanba's back arched as he screamed in pain.

"Kan-chan! It's okay! You'll be okay, Kan-chan!"

Himari pulled back slightly. Then she reached up, looking directly into his eyes, and cupped his face with both hands. His blood fell onto her forehead, cheeks, and the bare skin beneath her shredded nightgown. But she kept staring at him, unblinking.

It was Kanba who first suggested we repaint the wall of our house. I was originally against the idea. We were already social pariahs; I didn't want us to draw even *more* attention to ourselves. But Kanba said he didn't care what anyone else thought—he just wanted to make our house the kind of place Himari would always want to come home to, no matter what it took. He told me if it caused any problems, he would handle it himself.

Looking back, that was probably the moment that I finally acknowledged Kanba as my older brother. Somehow I sensed that he was willing to stand up and protect us. After that, things stopped being awkward between the three of us. Calling Kanba "Aniki" felt natural—comfortable, even. Over a long, long time, we gradually became real siblings, and after that, we were a real family.

"Kan-chan! Kan-chan!" Himari wiped the blood from his cheek and smiled. "You've done enough, Kan-chan. You don't have to go this far."

At her voice, Kanba stopped wailing. The light was returning to his eyes—the same headstrong eyes I remembered so fondly.

By now the majority of Himari's world was stained red, and it had already reached my feet. But I stepped into that pool of blood without hesitation. They were so close.

"See? It doesn't hurt, does it?"

No, it didn't hurt. It wasn't sad or scary. I accepted and loved Kanba as my brother, and he probably loved me, too. This was not a punishment meant for one person alone.

His blood formed dozens of bright red apples that rose up into the white fabric world, one by one. Then they formed an even bigger circle around the circle of teddy bears and slowly began to rotate.

"Himari..." It was Kanba's voice, without a doubt.

"Kan-chan! It's you! Welcome home."

Himari smiled brightly, then collapsed on the spot. Kanba caught her and wiped the blood off her face with his palm. Gently, he ran a finger over the cut on her forehead. Only then did I finally reach them; I doubled over, gasping for breath.

"I had a lot of fun all these years," I grinned. "Thank you, Kanba. I'll give you back everything you gave me—including the life you shared with me."

Gingerly, I pulled out the precious treasure burning brightly in my chest.

"We'll share it all—our love *and* our punishment."

As Kanba stared blankly back at me, I reached out with one hand and wiped the blood from his forehead.

"Kan-chan," Himari whispered up at him as she held him. "Look! See? This is the Penguindrum."

The borrowed life in my hand changed shape into half of an apple.

"You remember this, right, Aniki?"

His eyes widened as he looked at me. "Shoma..."

Sure enough, it was the voice of the Kanba we knew.

Back in that wooden cage, I was meant to die because I wasn't one of the chosen. But then Kanba split his apple in half and reached out through the bars of his cage as far as he could stretch in order to give it to me.

"Kanba...?" Wearily, I looked at him through the bars.

He nodded firmly, then stretched out even farther. Likewise, I reached out to him, attempting to take the other half of the apple. I was sure my fingers would reach. I was going to survive—he was giving me half of his life.

That was the moment Kanba chose me, and together, we shared the fruit of fate.

The next thing I knew, I was back on the subway train, sitting on the floor. Hastily, I jumped to my feet. Previously Kanba was standing next to Sanetoshi, but now he was at Himari's bedside, cradling her in her unscathed nightgown and penguin hat. She was hugging her beloved pink teddy bear to her chest.

"Let's share the fruit of fate!"

Oginome-san's shrill voice rang out across the train car. Covering my ears, I whirled around and saw her face to face with Sanetoshi, her shoulders heaving. Then the entire train began to rattle like there was an earthquake, and the black teddy bears fell off their seats one by one. Likewise, Oginome-san hit the floor. I moved toward her, but the train pitched sideways, and as the teddy bears rolled around, their color changed to white.

She successfully recited the fate transfer spell. The penguin hat slipped off Himari's head and fell to the floor. Sanetoshi looked at us, his expression twisted in pain.

"The transfer of fate will now begin," said a calm, pre-recorded voice over the intercom. "For those who wish to transfer, please head directly to the opposite platform to ensure you do not miss your next train."

I sucked in a breath and looked up.

"As a result of the incantation, a penalty will now be incurred. Please keep a safe distance from your fellow passengers."

"Oginome-san!"

But before I could finish, her body burst into flames.

So I dove into the fire and wrapped my arms around her.

As the train of fate pulled into the next station to facilitate the transfer, there was already another train waiting on the opposite side—perfectly ordinary from the looks of it. Kanba deboarded, carrying Himari in his arms. Then he crossed the platform to the other train, stepped aboard, and laid her down on the empty seats. He touched the one small cut left on Himari's large forehead and wished he could put an adhesive bandage on it, just like she'd always done for him.

"The transfer of fate will soon conclude. If you wish to transfer, please hurry to the next train immediately."

At the announcement, Kanba looked up. Then he rose to his feet, stepped off Himari's train, and slowly backed away across the platform until he returned to the train of fate.

"You kids will never be able to escape the curse. Nor can I," Sanetoshi declared smugly, his long white jacket fluttering behind him as he wandered aimlessly through the train car. He seemed restless. "You'll never gain anything as long as you're stuck in your little boxes! Every last trace of this world is going to disappear. There will be *nothing left*!"

His voice echoed as he stepped down onto the platform. But Kanba couldn't seem to hear him anymore. Eventually, he began to melt into the background like fog.

"You kids will never find true happiness."

Shoma cradled Ringo's burned body, and for the first time, he realized just how soft and supple she was. She looked at him, pain in her eyes, but her resolve was unwavering and beautiful. She couldn't speak; all she could do was blink at him.

"Oginome-san, thank you, but...this is our punishment to bear. I love you," he told her gently. Then he kissed her scorching hot lips. All at once, the flames moved from her body to his, burning ever brighter.

"Shoma-kun!"

Freed from the heat and pain, Ringo tried to pull away from him. She knew he was going to try to take her off the train of fate. But nevertheless, he lifted her up with what little strength he had left.

"Shoma-kun, stop! Let go!"

The edges of his shoulders were burning away to ash.

"Shoma-kun, you jerk! Stop! Let me go! I'm coming with you! I already decided I'm going to accept the punishment!"

But no matter how hard she struggled, Shoma simply grinned back. "This is goodbye. Now make sure you go get on that other train."

Smiling softly, Shoma set Ringo down on the platform. Then the automatic doors slid shut, and the train chime played, signaling its imminent departure. She collapsed on the spot; her mouth opened, but no words came. As she ruminated on the soft sensation lingering on her lips, she gazed into the train car at the flames burning inside.

Shoma and Kanba sat side by side on Himari's empty bed as they, the white teddy bears, and the bed itself burned up in the fire. All of it was slowly being written out of existence.

"Shoma, I finally found what true hope looks like," Kanba said softly.

"Yeah, I know. I saw it too, you know," Shoma snickered.

Then the burning train started moving. It glittered like a shooting star as it carried the boys off to a different fate, leaving the girls behind on the path to life.

Ringo staggered onto the remaining train and plopped down next to Himari as she slept. Then she reached out and stroked her long hair.

"Shoma-kun..."

What would happen to her feelings after the transfer was finished?

Then the train doors closed, and it quietly rolled out of the station, guiding them to a new destiny.

On the empty platform sandwiched between two sets of deserted train tracks, a defeated Sanetoshi stood alone, his hands stuffed into his jacket pockets, unmoving.

"Hey." It was Momoka who called out to him, holding two empty penguin hats in her hands. "The trains are gone, you know."

She walked up to him and looked up at his face with her big, round eyes. He met her gaze, but didn't smile.

"They'll be back eventually." Sanetoshi withdrew a hand from his pocket and ran it through his long hair. But his glossy locks had no appeal here in the dark.

"If you say so. Well, I'm gonna go now," she declared matter-of-factly.

"Right," he replied in a detached voice.

"If you want to come with me, I'll show you the way." She offered her hand.

"Goodbye," he answered without a single second of consideration.

She sighed and retracted her hand. "Goodbye then." And with that, she turned and walked away.

Standing stock-still on the hard asphalt of the platform, Sanetoshi let out a heavy sigh that resounded through the darkness. His breath chased after Momoka, glowing ever so faintly, but ultimately it failed to reach her.

PENGUINDRUM

CHAPTER 07

I AWOKE TO THE SOUNDS OF CHAOS all around me. As I opened my eyes, I came face to face with another girl just waking up. I had no idea who she was, but apparently we had passed out on the subway platform while holding hands. I was wearing a white nightgown, and she was wearing the uniform from the local all-girls' school.

"Hey! They're hurt! Somebody call an ambulance!" shouted a distant voice.

"Are you girls all right?"

Who? You mean her and me?

I closed my eyes again. I was really, *really* tired; I didn't have the energy to sit up and find out who this other girl was. Plus, my forehead ached, which suggested I was indeed injured.

It felt like the two of us had held hands the entire time we were unconscious. In reality, however, we were probably taken to the hospital in two separate ambulances.

When I finally awoke, it was just before dawn. I moved my stiff limbs and took stock of the bandages applied to my body. My forehead stung again, and when I reached up to touch it, I could feel gauze taped to the right side. Beside the bed, there were signs that I'd been put on a drip; on the bedside table was a bottle of green tea.

I sat up slightly. I was in a four-person hospital room, but the bed across from mine was curtained off, and the other two were empty. My gaze followed the streaming moonlight to the window. It was dark outside, save for the cherry blossoms glowing white.

How long had I been asleep? I hopped down out of bed and walked to the window. It was faintly chilly; I wrapped my arms around myself and gazed out at the cherry blossom petals falling like rain.

I had distant memories of a world blanketed in pure white snow—or was it just my imagination? Was it snow or ice? Was it chiffon or lace or satin? All I remembered was that everything was white and not nearly as cold as it looked.

The round yellow moon shone brightly against the faintly warm canvas of the night sky, illuminating my entire body as if I were in the process of photosynthesis.

"You're going to make yourself sick, you know."

My heart skipped a beat, and I whirled around. A girl with a bob cut was standing there in the moonlight, wearing pajamas and a pair of fuzzy slippers. It was the occupant of the bed across from mine—the same girl who was found lying unconscious next to me. Under her thick bangs, her defiant eyes glittered in the light.

"I was just distracted by the cherry blossoms," I told her, averting my gaze. "I'm sorry... Did I wake you?"

"No, no, not at all. But when I woke up and saw this girl with super-long hair standing at the window, I was like, 'Is this a dream?' Glad to know you're not a ghost, at least." She laughed amiably. "I'm Oginome Ringo."

"Ikebe Himari. Nice to meet you."

Truth be told, this introduction was a little belated, considering they had already technically "met" at Ikebukuro Station... although it still wasn't clear why they had both passed out next to each other.

"Do we know each other?" Oginome Ringo-san asked, tilting her head slightly as she stood beside me, gazing out the window.

"No, I don't think so." Out in the chilly night air, the cherry blossom petals looked like warm feathers.

"Yeah, I don't think I know you. But the funny thing is...for some reason, I'm *glad* that I woke up next to you. I don't know why, but it came as a relief." She was smiling so brightly, I couldn't help but smile along with her.

"Call me Himari."

"Okay then, you can call me Ringo."

After that, the two of us stood side by side, absently gazing out at the flowers in full bloom. In my mind, I tried to retrace the memory of that biting cold winter, but again and again, I kept losing the thread partway through. And I probably wasn't the only one trying to piece it together, either.

We stood there for a long time, admiring the big cherry blossom tree from the safety of our dark hospital room...until a nurse came and scolded us, that is.

"Good night," I told Ringo-chan as I climbed back into bed.

"Night night. See you tomorrow."

She felt like an old friend—the kind of close friend whose hand I wanted to hold while I was falling asleep. In the end, I fell into a deep, dreamless slumber.

Tokikago Yuri was at peace, bundled up in the blanket Tabuki Keiju brought for her. They sat in a living room far too large for just the two of them, but nevertheless, it was furnished with comfort in mind. Here at the top of the high-rise condo building, they could get a clear view of the entire city through the windows.

"It's been a long time since I last had the chance to sit back and enjoy the cherry blossoms," Tabuki murmured absently.

Compared to Yuri, who had spent her adult life swamped with acting gigs, Tabuki surely would have had plenty of opportunities to go on a hanami picnic. She gazed at his unremarkable face— his tacky thick-rimmed glasses, his shaggy hair that he refused to go have cut, and his kind, hardworking vibe. But it was precisely that unremarkable quality that they truly needed in their lives.

"Same here. I'm glad we have this condo."

Soft orange light enveloped the living room, and as they sat there next to the tall windows with their custom-ordered curtains, Yuri fit perfectly into Tabuki's arms. They weren't just embracing each other—they were keeping each other upright, like any other married couple. Meanwhile, the cherry blossom trees glowed ghostly white, their petals falling here and there. It was then that they both remembered the promise they made with Momoka to one day look at the cherry blossoms as a trio.

"Yuri, I finally realized why we were the only ones who survived."

She could feel his large, warm hands through the blanket as he wrapped his arms around her.

"And why is that?"

She breathed a sigh of relief. Perhaps she belonged here; perhaps this was where she was meant to be. The thought made her feel secure...and drowsy.

"You and I were lost children right from the start—but in this world, most children are. That's why I needed someone to tell me they loved me, even just once."

"That makes sense."

Even if fate had stolen everything from them—even if the words and memories disappeared—children who knew love would one day find happiness again. What Momoka left behind for them had helped lead them to this conclusion.

"That's why we were left behind."

"Classic Tabuki-kun." She smiled quietly. "I really love you."

"I love you, too." *And everything you've ever loved,* he added silently.

Neither of them had lived perfect, pristine lives, but their fates were deeply entwined, bringing them together in the end. Yuri's loose curls swayed as she reached out from under the blanket, searching for his hand. She found it near his stomach and grasped it firmly.

"Yuri, you're freezing," Tabuki murmured on reflex, concerned.

"No, *you're* just burning up," she shot back, pouting.

With a wry smile, Tabuki decided to make a cup of tea for his cold-sensitive wife. It was nothing fancy, but it was warm.

Setting aside the hospital's carefully regulated air conditioning, I was pretty sure everything was colder before I suffered that bizarre accident. Right now, however, the sky above the courtyard was clear and blue, like someone painted it with a single stroke of their paintbrush; every time the wind rustled the branches on the cherry blossom trees, more petals rained down onto my lap.

The doctor was worried I suffered some sort of memory loss, so they ran a bunch of tests, but ultimately couldn't find any problems. But it wasn't just me—neither my aunt nor my uncle could tell me why I had gone to Ikebukuro Station in the first place.

"Himari-chan!"

I could see Ringo-chan racing over to me in her blue polka-dot pajamas, reminiscent of soap bubbles. Smiling, I adjusted the hem of my peach-pink nightgown. Over the past three days since we first arrived at this hospital, the two of us became fast friends. She was an outgoing girl slightly older than me whose biggest talent was making curry.

"Hi, Ringo-chan. How'd it go?" I asked casually. Neither of us was worried about the results of our tests.

"Zilch. I'm as fit as a fiddle, they said!"

She struck a victory pose, and I giggled. Other than the cut on my forehead and the light burn on her back, there were no clues explaining how we had passed out.

"Were you admiring the cherry blossoms?" she asked as she sat down next to me.

"Yup."

Silence fell between us for a moment.

"Will you teach me how to knit? Although I guess it's getting a little too warm to be wearing scarves anyhow." She reached out and scooped up a fallen petal.

"I don't mind. As long as *you* teach me how to make a good curry."

There was a lot we still didn't know about each other, but we didn't mind at all. In fact, we suspected that perhaps fate had brought us together at Ikebukuro.

"I'm gonna need to pack up soon. My aunt and uncle are coming to get me," I murmured absently.

"Me, too. My mom said she's gonna leave work early to pick me up."

We both had our own separate lives to get back to, but somehow it felt so natural, watching TV and flipping through magazines together. It was strange to think I'd be going back to a life without her—and I was sure she felt the same way—but I didn't know how to convey it in words. On a whim, I reached up and touched the wound on my forehead. Under the big adhesive bandage was a series of sutures that were scheduled to be removed in a few days' time.

"The flowers are really pretty."

Unwilling to get up just yet, I turned my attention back to the trees.

"Yeah."

The petals were starting to pile up in *her* lap, too.

Natsume Masako sat on a bench in the gazebo out behind the mansion, and believe it or not, she was dozing off. The lukewarm breeze was caressing her curls, and the book she was holding was threatening to slip right out of her hands. Each time her head slumped, she lost track of whether the gentle touch she felt was reality or a dream.

"Oneesama?" Her younger brother Mario, who was playing in the yard, came over and peered at her. "You can't sleep out here or you'll get sick."

Masako snapped back to her senses and stared intently at the boy in front of her. He was smiling slightly, and his palms were covered in mud.

"Oh...y-yes, you're right." Adjusting her curls with one hand, she straightened her posture. Spring came swiftly this year, and it was already too warm for a coat.

"Mario-san, are you feeling all right?"

"Huh? What are you talking about, Oneesama?" He tilted his head.

"It's nothing, don't worry. Goodness, my mind must be playing tricks on me. Must have been that dream I had." She looked at the cherry blossom petals piled at her feet.

"What kind of dream?" Mario asked, toying with his muddy hands.

"A very strange dream indeed. It was freezing cold, and our older brother was there," she laughed, amused at the absurdity of her statement.

"What older brother?"

"My twin."

"Hmmm... So he was just like you?" Mario asked, eyes sparkling with curiosity.

"No, not at all. He was a clumsy, clueless person. He would always put himself on the back burner, and he would never outright ask for the attention he so craved. But deep down, he always remembered the words that mattered most."

The top of her head felt vaguely warm, right in the spot where his hand had touched her during the dream.

"But at the very least, he told me he loved and cherished me as his one and only sister."

"Are you crying, Oneesama?" Hastily, Mario reached into the pocket of his corduroy shorts and pulled out a handkerchief... instantly soiling it with his muddy fingers. "Oh...sorry..."

"That's all right. I wonder what's gotten into me..." Masako wiped her tears away with her fingers and let out a heavy sigh. "Now go wash your hands. It's time for our afternoon tea."

"Okay!" he answered cheerfully, then raced off into the house.

Filled with the strangest feeling of contentment, Masako felt as though she was blessed with all the world's compassion.

In terms of personality, he was nothing like her, but they

both shared the same sharp eyes. That said, she didn't actually have a twin brother at all—so why would she dream about one? Evidently it was something her subconscious needed.

Today, she would brew a pot of Nuwara Eliya to celebrate the fresh green of spring. Then, while they ate Mario's favorite cookies, she would tell him a bit more about the older brother from her dream. And as she spoke, she would stroke his hair...just as her "brother" had done for her.

I lived in an old one-story house in a fairly safe part of Ogikubo. The most striking thing about it was its rusty metal siding; my uncle claimed he was thinking about replacing it, but that was years ago by this point. Besides, I enjoyed the sound of the rain pattering against it whenever there was a storm, so I wasn't in any huge rush to have it renovated. It was unique, and it held up well, even after its protective coating was worn away.

My room was slightly cramped, with a small study desk and a wardrobe for my clothes. Next to the desk was an old bookshelf full of novels and manga, some of them mine, some of them my uncle's. There were cushions on the floor, plus some stuffed animals, a CD player and a handful of CDs, yarn balls, buttons and ribbons, thimbles, spools of thread, and a pincushion of needles... oh, and my fashion magazines.

I put all my sewing equipment back into its little pink basket, then pulled off my navy blue uniform jacket. With one hand reaching for the buttons of my blouse, I opened the wardrobe.

My dinner was already on the stove; I just needed to give it a few minutes to simmer. "Now then," I muttered as I returned to the kitchen and pulled my apron back on over my loungewear: a pale purple-checkered dress featuring a smocked chest panel, puffy sleeves, and a balloon skirt.

I peered into the pot.

"We mustn't rush, my dear. At such a high temperature, why, you might get burned!" I said in a theatrical voice, cackling evilly. "Wicked girl. You brought this upon yourself, I'm afraid."

Rolling up my long sleeves, I stirred the thickly bubbling curry with a ladle. Then I scooped some up for a taste test. This was the Oginome family recipe, taught to me by none other than Ringo-chan herself.

"Yes, it's perfect!"

I set my ladle down on the cooktop and put the lid on the pot. Now I just needed to wait until Ringo-chan arrived. Then, as I was cleaning the coffee table, the phone rang.

"Hello? Uncle Ikebe? Oh, you'll be home late? Both of you? Sure, that's fine. I'm having a friend over for lunch, so I made curry. You guys can have some later tonight when you get back." Next to the phone was a framed photograph of me with my aunt and uncle, taken on the first day of school. "Yeah, Ringo-chan, the girl from the hospital. Don't worry, she'll keep me company."

As I set the receiver back down, I let out a sigh. After I finished cleaning the table, I was out of things to do.

In this house, the living room was brimming with things I collected: toys hanging from the light cords, stickers on the tissue box cover, embroidery on the red curtains that I periodically added to over the years, merch from my beloved Double H, and some awards I got as a child. My aunt and uncle weren't actually biologically related to me, but I was living with them for as long as I could remember. They were a childless couple, and they treated me with as much love and care as their confectionery. Thus, I had never tried to track down my real parents. All I knew was that something serious had happened to them, but they weren't bad people; I was their only child, and they loved me. That was everything there was to know about me.

Quietly, I decided to break out the confectionery once Ringo-chan arrived. Then the sound of the doorbell brought me back to my senses, and I rose to my feet.

"Coming!"

Ringo-chan took a big whiff of the rising steam and smiled brightly. The table was decked out with two plates of curry, two simple side salads, and two cups of tea.

"Mmmm, looks good!" she exclaimed. She stopped by on her way home from school, so she was wearing her uniform.

We pressed our hands together to say grace. Then I watched carefully as she took her first bite.

"How is it?"

"It's good! Your cooking skills have really leveled up, Himari-chan!"

Today was the 20th of the month, which Ringo-chan tradition-ally designated "Curry Day." I didn't know why. Maybe she would tell me someday, or maybe she wouldn't; I didn't mind either way.

It felt like fate had brought the two of us together. First we passed out at the same subway station, then we were taken to the same hospital, and then we made friends so quickly, you'd think we'd met before. If anything had the right to be called fate, it was this.

"All thanks to your awesome recipe, Ringo-chan." Relieved, I took a bite myself.

"Isn't it great?! The grated apple really adds something!" she exclaimed, thrusting her chest out proudly.

"Oh, I just remembered—Double H is on TV today!" With a grin, I switched on the television.

"Right, yeah. Gosh, they're so cute!"

We watched as the duo in question popped onscreen and started to sing. The two of us were both Double H superfans, and we liked to collect all their albums and merch—cartoony key chains, little plushies, calendars, and pins.

"Ooh, it's their new single," Ringo-chan murmured. She was more of a Hikari-chan fan, if she had to choose.

"Wanna listen to their new album? I'll go get it," I told her as I rose to my feet. If *I* had to pick, I was more of a Hibari-chan gal.

I walked into my room, over to the corner with the plushies and sewing tools, and crouched down. My CDs weren't on the bookshelf; I kept them in a flower-print shoebox.

"Wait, where are they?"

I looked around for the box. It occurred to me I might have left it on my desk, so I started to straighten up...but then I spotted my pink teddy bear. He was dressed up like a pirate, complete with bandana and eyepatch, and I had cherished him since I was a kid.

"Oh, his tummy stitching is coming loose…"

Tempted to fix it, I reached out and grabbed him. Then, as I sat him on my lap, I saw something else poking out through the seam—something that looked like a scrap of paper. Gently, I pinched it between my fingers and pulled it out. Sure enough, it was an old, yellowed piece of paper; I unfolded it to find the clumsy writing of a child.

To Himari: We'll always love you. Love, your big brothers.

"Big brothers?"

Who could that be? It felt like a vise clamped down on my heart. I had no recollection of any brothers.

"Himari-chan?" a voice called from behind me. I looked over my shoulder to find Ringo-chan standing there, her eyes wide. "What's wrong?"

"Look at this." The next thing I knew, I was crying, but I couldn't explain why. Instead, I looked back down at the little note in my hand. "This is so bizarre… What's gotten into me…?"

"What's going on? Himari-chan, are you okay?" Ringo-chan rushed over to me, crouched down beside me, and pulled me into a hug.

"I don't get it…" Tears kept rolling down my face, and I started to sob. "Why am I crying…?"

"It's all right. I'm right here with you," she told me reassuringly, like a big sister.

"Yeah, I know... I'm sorry, Ringo-chan." Confused, I buried my face in her shoulder.

"It's okay." She stroked my hair softly, over and over. "We'll always be together."

Naturally, this made me cry even harder.

I really appreciated my life with my aunt and uncle, and I appreciated that Ringo-chan was a part of it. I was happy being a fan of Double H, and getting better at making curry. And I loved my pink teddy bear and the mystery note that was hiding inside him. I loved the word "fate," and I believed from the bottom of my heart that I would never have to be alone.

Two young boys walked down the street, admiring the falling cherry blossom petals.

"No, see, the apple represents the whole universe, sitting right in the palm of your hand. It's the bridge between our world and the other world," said the first boy, a hint of exasperation in his voice, shielding his sharp eyes from the rays of sunlight streaming down through the branches of the cherry blossom trees.

"What other world?" asked the second, tilting his head as he plucked the petals off of his messy, wavy hair.

"The one Giovanni and Campanella and all the other passengers are going to," the first replied matter-of-factly, looking back at him.

"Okay, but where is it?" the second boy demanded, looking over his shoulder. Two chubby male penguins with round button eyes waddled after them.

"It's the place where all life comes from. And Campanella's mom is there, too."

The two penguins turned around and beckoned behind them to two *more* penguins, who rushed out from between the cherry blossom trees to join up with the rest of the group. The third penguin had sparkly eyes and was wearing a ribbon on its head; the fourth looked at the third with aloof, upturned eyes, then took her by the flipper and started waddling.

"But what does that have to do with apples?" asked the messy-haired boy, smiling at the third penguin.

"The apples are a gift from God," the other boy declared smugly.

The messy-haired boy scowled. "That makes no sense."

"In other words, they're a reward for the passengers who chose to die for love."

"But that's pointless. Once you die, your life is over."

"No it's not, dumbo. It's just the beginning. That's what Kenji's trying to say."

Just then, a strong wind blew past, and an avalanche of cherry blossom petals cascaded down upon the group.

"So where do we go from here?" the messy-haired boy asked, stopping to dust the petals from his hair with both hands.

"I dunno. Where do you *wanna* go? This is where it starts."

The other boy looked at the penguins following them and smirked. At some point the procession had grown, and now four petal-covered birds trailed them, all in a row.

There will be no more getting angry, or getting sad, or standing still. The two children will surely surpass time and space to revel in the freedom of joy and despair. They can go anywhere they want to go, or see anyone they want to see; they can celebrate their perpetual motion by singing at the top of their lungs. Supposing they did, the penguins would surely join in, their shrill little voices like that of four steam whistles.

Eventually the pale pink petals will become countless shining stars. Together with the big, bright moon, they will shine down gently upon everything worthy of love. The girl's tears will dry, and she'll fall fast asleep in a warm bed.

Rest assured, there's nothing to cry about. This journey will take us into the night sky, which means it will surely be a good one. And even if something bad *does* happen, we'll put our heads together and find a solution. That's what knowledge and language is for—to help us find happiness. At least, that's what we have to believe.

So what's the difference between life and the endless bounds of space? The fact that we existed lies within the never-ending cycle of life and death, fated never to disappear for almost eternity. See there, in that child's heart? Those memories will bear fruit and grant the power to imagine a new universe. Really, there's nothing to cry about. This is probably what love is.

Don't be afraid. Don't lose faith. Just look right into that person's eyes and tell them you love them, again and again, as many times as it takes to reach them.

THE END

PENGUINDRUM

AUTHOR BIOS

Kunihiko Ikuhara

Born December 21. Animation director. Made his directorial debut in 1993 while affiliated with Toei Animated Films (presently, Toei Animation), with *Pretty Guardian Sailor Moon R*. Achieved acclaim in 1997, with the debut of *Revolutionary Girl Utena*, which he independently planned and directed. The original author of manifold novels and manga.

Kei Takahashi

Born October 15, 1980, and raised in Tokyo.

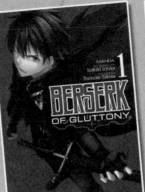